Downriver

by Erik Hare

authorHOUSE™

1663 LIBERTY DRIVE, SUITE 200
BLOOMINGTON, INDIANA 47403
(800) 839-8640
WWW.AUTHORHOUSE.COM

First published by AuthorHouse 10/07/05

ISBN: 1-4208-8716-5 (sc)

Library of Congress Control Number: 2005908936

Printed in the United States of America
Bloomington, Indiana

This book is printed on acid-free paper.

For George, who has his imagination.
For Kate, who always wants to help.

For Ellen, who inspired me.
For Watney, who taught me.
For Cristy, who encouraged me.

And for Julie, who makes me feel alive.

CONTENTS

40-3-17-34-13
63-64-29-28-43
15-53-8-78-20
26-48-47-27-23

Note on Translation

The story was originally told in the Hopneg language. Some of the names and terms do not translate directly, so the best available word was used. Wherever possible, exact descriptions are translated word for word.

The term "Prairie Gnome" is considered derogatory, and is only used as a direct quote. "Hopneg" is substituted in every other case, since this is what they call themselves.

The names "Lilly" and "Emily" are not the names they were born with, but the names they assumed in the Land of the Giants. They would not reveal their original names, so they are called what they want to be called.

Chapter 1:
By No Means

It started as an uncomfortable feeling.

Not really an event, but not quite a dream, the far off rumble snuck up gently. Popey didn't wake up right away. Instead, he flinched over on his side and under his grass pillow and then flat on his front as if he was rolling to get away. But it didn't work. The rumble finally got him.

Sitting up, Popey realized that he and everything he owned was now thumping up and down, and violently. He threw open his mouth to gasp in a breath of cool air. Instead, found that his heart had been thrown up into his throat, pulsing wildly to the throbbing beat of the closer and closer rumble.

He tossed off his covers and ran to the top of his tiny burrow on wobbly but determined legs, and nudged his head out to see what this could be. All he saw was a shining wall of metal boiling the ground before it, sometimes pounding angrily at the earth. It was heading right for him! With a bursting leap and a crawling run, Popey tumbled off to the side of this terrible Demon. It passed him by with a cloud of dust and foul smoke, leaving Popey flat on his back, and not sure if the world was upside down or not.

Only his thin white pajamas covered his three and a quarter inch tall body. He lay there a moment and panted in the settling, greasy air.

Popey had seen shiny metal Demons before, but they were never like this one. They were always much smaller, and only cut a shallow trench in the earth. Besides, even they had not been through this field for two whole years now. It was as if they had come back with a vengeance.

When the dust and smoke cleared, Popey rolled over to look. This Demon was much larger, with a huge yellow body behind the metal. It sucked in breath through its mouth with a whoosh and

1

belted out smoke from the top. And it left everything smooth and flat as it rumbled forward. When it was done, Popey's house and everything he owned had simply vanished.

There was only one thing to do now – get help from those who knew about these things. His older sister, Lilly, could help him find Rouger and the others who would know what to do. "Lilly will take care of me. This will work out." Each wobbly footstep that broke into a run brought a new thought that focused him on his journey. "So I lost everything. My friends will help. What was that horrible thing?" It took a long time to make it all the way across the field, but a strong potion of equal parts terror and hope that ran in his blood kept him moving.

Popey reached the end of the field, and glanced back just a moment. The Demon was at the far end, puffing and rumbling. The cooler air of the grove wrapped around him, pulling him in to its safety. He stumbled into it, wrenching his eyes away from the horror still happening.

"Popey? You're all right?" It was Lilly's voice that finally woke him from what he hoped was just a terrible dream. She stood before him in her beautiful aquamarine cloak with fur trim, her long dark braids snapped in place with jeweled berets. Her cobalt skirt was splattered with mud that betrayed her panic. She lunged forward and hugged him as if it were for the last time.

"Yes… Lilly!… ah, I'm fine. I lost… everything, but… I'm fine."
"Thank goodness you're all right. But you have nothing? You have no magic?"
Popey freed himself from Lilly's grip and plunked himself onto a branch.
"No, nothing… but I'm fine."
"But Popey, you have no magic anymore! What will you do?"

The reality finally hit Popey hard. Without any possessions, he had lost the magic of ownership completely. He had become a Punk, the lowest kind of Hopneg there is. He stared at Lilly for a moment not knowing what to tell her.
"Take this," Lilly told him, reaching into her broad black belt, "It's the staff that Mom gave to me before she died."

"No, I can't take that!"

"Take it!" Lilly yelled, "I won't have a brother who is a Punk! I'll take care of you, Popey."

What Popey hoped for more than anything as he tramped across the field, to have his older sister help him, was coming true. But it somehow made him feel worse than when he realized everything of his was gone. She already saw him as something less now that he had no magic of his own. If he took something from her, it would be fake, it would always be her magic.

"Let me sit down for a while. I can do this on my own."

As Popey withdrew, Lilly neatly concealed the small wooden staff back into her belt. Popey remained still on the branch, his head drooped into his hands. Lilly hesitated, but sat next to him with her waiting eyes frozen on her brother.

"Popey, you rest a bit, but we have to see Rouger as soon as we can and tell him."

"Tell him I'm a Punk?"

"What? No, tell him what's happening. You're not the only one who was out there when the snorting yellow Demon showed up!"

"Right. Did the others get out?"

The size of the event was still dawning on Popey. Lilly finally sat down next to him and spoke softly.

"No one else has gotten out, Popey. It, ah... we don't know what happened."

"What... is that Demon?" Popey asked.

"I... rest a while, we'll see Rouger. I don't know. Have a drink."

"Last time I sleep in, I swear..."

Lilly gave Popey a canteen of water she slipped from her belt, and he drank deeply. The cool water hit his hot throat in a hard but welcome splash. The excitement of the moment was cooled down in gulps that ran out as fast as they could. When it was empty, Popey very deliberately and carefully gave the canteen back to Lilly, who blushed a pale pink and put it away.

They said nothing for a long time, Lilly wondering if her brother was too much in shock to understand his situation. Not knowing what to do, she simply slid her arm around him and waited for his stare to get off the ground. She did not realize that inside Popey a strange new determination was brewing.

CHAPTER 2:
HUSHING

"Allright, let's go." When the words finally came they split the cool air and hung for a moment. Lilly, relieved that Popey seemed to be coming to his senses, stood as he did. "You sure you're fine?" "Yes, Lilly, I want to see what Rouger has to say about this." There was a hint of fight in his voice that did not make Lilly feel good. They started waking towards the big old oak at the center of the grove, the finest house of all the Hopnegs, before she tried to gently scold her little brother.

"Popey, remember your place. Things aren't what they were." "Huh?... my place, yes, I know. But he will remember who I am. Besides, you're still my sister, and he'll listen to you."

Counting on Lilly to pull him through came easily for him, since his sister was one of the most respected and wealthy food gatherers in the community. What Popey had forgotten, once again, was that this meant nothing for him.

"I am your sister," Lilly told him, "but now that you remember I can help you, would you please remember to let me help you?"

Their heavy footsteps took them to a small clearing where a large crowd murmured. Several of them saw Popey coming, and greeted him warmly. One young girl in a flowing pink dress ran up to give him a flying hug around his waist. A few others, however, took one look at his dirty white pajamas and jerked their heads away, as if not wanting to see an accident happen. To the right, a plainly dressed man had a cart from which he was selling freshly roasted seeds. Lilly bought Popey a handful which he ate greedily. At least he had breakfast.

Wiping his chin, Popey was just finishing the story of the Demon with the wall of metal to some of the crowd when a great big door in the oak beyond opened. A hush stilled the crowd in waves, leaving space for the barked announcement – "The Lord Mayor, Rouger".

A large Hopneg wearing an attention grabbing blue pinstripe suit with an oversized fur collar stepped out. He was large and handsome, his full frame topped by a nearly bald head framed with a wreath of curly hair. On his front, his suit was buttoned together with a large jewel. At his side was a large vole leashed to his side through a fine leather collar with sparkling jewels all around it. He spoke without pause:

"Citizens, greetings. First, a moment of silence please for those who have perished." Two hundred heads bowed, and suddenly a few gentle sniffles were the only sound that cut the breeze. After a while, Rouger continued, "Today's events have saddened us beyond words, but as we remember those who have fallen let us not forget that we are a proud race who can, and will, endure. In times like this, we must not let our honest and true emotions overcome us. We must learn to rely on our cleverness and those who are the wisest among us. And we will find a way out of this situation. Today's events, I am sad to report, are the work of the Giants."

With this last sentence, the crowd became restless again. The words "Giants!" and "I knew it!" and a few not very nice words bubbled through the air.

Rouger continued, "Calm down, calm down. We still have information to gather and decisions to make. As The Book says, 'Place your first step well, for it determines which direction you go'. We will find a way through this. But first, I need the assistance of a young man who is both fleet of foot and clear in mind. Misha, would you explain to them?"

An older woman stepped up, wearing a simple red robe that was elegant but plain. Her wispy white hair was pulled back in a bun that seemed to be trying to pull the weathered lines from her face. She stood on a small box next to Rouger and addressed the crowd with a high, clear voice that grabbed their ears.

"There is a signpost at the edge of the field, posted by the Giants. It may contain words that describe what is happening. We need to know what is on that sign, so we can determine what to do next. A young man who can run there and back quickly, and remember what it says, will earn our eternal gratitude."

The crowd bubbled noisily again, since it was well known that only the very powerful could read actual words. How would a simple child handle this task? But a young man nearly of age to be a Citizen rose, and stepped forward to give it a try.

"A brave man you are," Rouger greeted him, "For we need you well in this dire moment. If you cannot remember all the words you see, be sure to remember the big ones. The Giants use a lot of small words to fill in space, but it is the big words that carry magic from the very most powerful of their kind."

With that, the young Hopneg sprinted off to the edge of the field, and was soon out of sight. The crowd began to turn slightly, but Rouger pulled them back to enjoy their favor once more.

"Citizens, remain steadfast. At times like these, we need our great wisdom more than ever. As The Book says, 'The clever can win a race against even the fastest of runners'. We will let you know when we understand better what manner of Demon we are up against. Until then, patience will have to suit us all. Good day."

And with that he turned around and slipped back through the door of his tree root house, thudding it closed. Popey turned to Lilly and said in a whisper, "He doesn't have a clue, does he!" Lilly was taken aback by this comment, and shot an angry look at her brother, "He has The Book, and it's guided us ever since the Giants arrived. What else do we have to use in a... a situation like this?"

Popey wanted to argue, but he had no idea how to. He had seen this Demon up close, and he knew this was something very different. If Rouger was making a decision, he needed to know what they were up against. Popey had to talk to him, to tell his story. But rather than argue with his sister, he fumbled and stared at the ground. He decided instead to ask her for more money for roasted seeds. Suddenly, a flash of red to his left settled this kick of hunger.

The frail figure of Misha came through the crowd, and Lilly greeted her with the hug of an old friend. "Misha, dear, how lovely to see you again, terrible time we have." Misha patted Lilly on the back, and spoke warmly. "Yes, dear child, something awful is happening, but we will get through it." She then turned to Popey, or half turned, and whispered as if she were his mother, "Popey, do not worry, my child. You will be taken care of. There will be a lot of work to do, and you will have new magic of your own. Please stop and see me later. There will be something for you, child."

The words warmed Popey, but not being addressed directly made him feel that the term of endearment, "child", was eating into him like acid. He did not know what do to or say, but somewhere in the pit of his guts the words bubbled out, "Thank you... Lilly, can I have some more money for seeds?" Lilly gave him the small coins with a relief on all sides – that Lilly could talk with Misha and Popey could have a decent escape from the situation. He felt like a kid, and for some reason he did not mind acting like one. It suited him at the moment.

On the way back from grabbing his snack, he passed a few other Hopnegs he knew well. They mostly turned their eyes aside, preferring to not see him. Only one, Rodele, took the time to greet him and ask how he got out. "You made it! What happened out there?" And as Popey recounted the tale for what seemed like the millionth time, he fell into a patter like the retelling of an ancient legend. But Rodele seemed genuinely impressed.

"Popey, you're still a strong and smart young man. You can be depended on, and I know this well." The words were the first encouragement he'd gotten since he rolled away from the Demon. He made a note to seek out Rodele when things settled a bit, to see what he could make of his life after losing everything.

"Thanks, Rod, you're a real friend."
"Popey, whatever you need... just find me. We can do great things together."
"Ah, yeah... I'm sure we can. Thanks."

Just then, they were interrupted by a wave of silence that came over the gathered crowd, which was greeting the young man sent off to run to the large sign. He arrived in a panting stumble, clearly having run like he had never run before. As he gasped for air, Misha made her way over and tended to him, and the great door opened again to reveal the figure of Rouger.

The crowd extended a friendly arm that gave him a canteen full of water, which he downed in one gulp. He squatted like a hurt warrior while Misha put her arm around him and asked him, gently, "What did you see, child?" The young Hopneg said nothing, but took a stick by his side and scratched into the dirt:

TOWNHOMES

Rouger cleared his throat, not knowing what to say. Misha spoke up and said with determination, "It is as I feared. The Giants have claimed this for their homes. They have a magic that we do not, for they can own the land itself."

A voice from the crowd called out, "How can they own land?" Another asked, "What kind of magic is this?" So Misha continued, "This is a powerful magic. It is the kind of magic that calls forth Demons like we have seen. We Hopnegs own only what we can carry, but the Giants own the very land. This has been our bane ever since they arrived. This is why The Book was written. But child, were there any other words you remember?"

"Only... one more. You said... to remember the big words," he panted out. "This... was the biggest... of all". And he took the stick and scratched into the dirt again.

SUBIVISION

Those in the crowd that could see it gasped slightly. They could not read, but the sign had so many large words there was clearly some powerful magic at work. Rouger, who was clearly at a loss for what to say, was uncomfortably not in control of the situation. He asked Misha, quietly, "What does this mean?"

"I am not sure, either, Rouger." Misha told him, "The word 'vision' means sight or seeing, and 'sub' means below. This is happening below sight, or without being seen. Perhaps this is a warning to the other Giants not to look, or else the spell is broken."

Rouger paid little attention to this, his eyes betraying the vacant look of a man trying to think his way out of a situation. After a long time, he spoke up in the deepest voice he could pull out.

"Citizens, listen carefully, for I fear that our time in the River Flats is ending. We have been fat and happy for a long time, but that time is over. We should not fear it, but allow it to lead us on to greater things. Do not forget what is written in The Book, 'Hopnegs are fueled by their desires and their ambitions, and can accomplish much by their own interests'. As we must move on, our inventiveness will drive us on to a better world. New places mean new things for us to find and harvest. Life will be better, though we must not allow ourselves to be this fat and happy again."

The last sentence may have been too much, for the crowd was murmuring. Popey, however, felt a red haze boil up in front of his eyes and into his brain, and finally into his throat.

"That makes no sense! We can defeat this Demon, but only if we stop being selfish and work together for once!"

Popey had no idea where that voice came from. It was as if something had taken possession of him. The crowd bubbled slightly, a few of them turning for a quick look at the one who dared talk like this. But Rouger pretended that nothing had happened.

"Our cleverness has always helped us to find a way around the Giants in the past, and it will serve us again. We must move on, but we will move on to a better place. We will move away from the Giants, and further out to the countryside. The Book says, 'Plenty of space so that you cannot see the Giants that live around you is the home you should seek', and we will seek that."

"This is our home!" Popey felt the words come from inside, beyond his thinking. He wondered why this didn't scare him. But aside from a few glances, the crowd was unmoved. Rouger continued to pretend that Popey didn't exist.

"Our magic is limited, our possessions small, but we can find a rich land far from the Giants where there is much more magic to be had."

"Look at that Demon! The sign says don't look, so look! There are other kinds of magic!" Popey didn't care about anything anymore.

"SILENCE, YOU PUNK!"

Rouger finally acknowledged Popey in a purple fit of rage. The crowd was now bubbling in a wordy broth that was angry and confused. And out of the corner of his eye, Popey saw Lilly running over to him.

"Popey, stop that, now! Let's get you out of here!"
"Lilly, why? Someone has to say something! We can't move!"
"Why... would you go against the wisdom of the book? What on earth... what do you want? Come on, let's go."

Popey allowed himself to be pulled by the arm away from the clearing and into the thick part of the woods, where they could hide behind a sapling and talk privately for a while. His anger fell slowly, but was still there below where he could see it. He could talk to Lilly calmly. They both sat on a small twig while Popey waved his arms frantically.

"Lilly, he's just giving up! They're all giving up! What's so clever about that? Why can't we work together to stop this?"
"Oh, Popey... can't you see that we need more magic if we're going to fight this? We just don't have the... power to do it. Rouger doesn't want to say it out loud, but he doesn't have it. He's trying to make it sound better, but he's as scared as all of us."
"But there are other kinds of magic! I can feel it, even though I have no magic of my own, that there's a different kind – like that Demon!"
"If Rouger doesn't have the power to fight that, who does?"
"I don't know... maybe we all do?"

Lilly let that last comment settle from the air a moment before she put her arm around Popey like a big sister. "Popey, you know I've worked really hard, and I'm proud of the magic I've got. It's difficult, terrible work, but I have learned many things. And one thing that I've learned is that all of the magic we gather is only worth so much. We are, after all, very small creatures."

11

Popey glanced over at her. "We're only small because they are big."

He had no idea where this comment came from, but he had learned to let these things come out. There was something bottled up inside, and he felt better every time it leaked out a little bit. He liked it as it hung in the air.

"What?" Lilly asked him. "Of course, but... that's why we have to be so careful. Why do you... what does that mean?"
"It means what it says. We are only small because we compare ourselves to them. We see their magic and think we can't have it. I don't know why that... why it has to be true."

He stopped a moment, but Lilly wasn't in this conversation with him. He continued, "I've done what I was told for a long time. I don't mind being your little brother, but I don't want to be your little brother. I don't mind doing things for other people, but I don't want to do things for other people. I nearly died today, and I'm really happy to be alive. And all anyone can do is look at me like losing everything is worse than death, that I should have died. But... I didn't die, I lived. I live. I just don't want to do what I'm told anymore... well, not all the time. You see?... I didn't die..."

The last sentence hung in the air like the dust stirred up by the Demon. He lost his train of thought as the deep red feeling drained from him. Lilly saw it go from his eyes, but still felt the heavy presence around them, 'I didn't die'. Her head felt heavy as she realized she had forgotten something important.

"Popey, my brother. Words are failing us both. I think I know what you mean, and... I'm sorry, I should have let you know how happy I am you're alive. I really am. You've been a good brother and I just didn't... you work too hard for people to think you're a Punk, is all. I..."

But she still didn't understand. "Lilly, it's not about all the time I spent milking dandelions or harvesting seeds for you. It's about being..."
"You're more than that, I know, I'm just..."

"Something happened inside of me, Lilly. That's what .."
"You're in shock, Popey."
"No, well… maybe, but it feels… great!"

Lilly finally lifted her head to take a long look into Popey's deep black eyes. And she understood what he was talking about. Something was new in there, something she hadn't seen before. He wasn't just the shy, quiet little brother she had been taking care of since their mother died.

Another long pause let her change the subject to something she was more comfortable with. "Popey, it's been a long day. Maybe you should get a nice hot meal and go to bed early. I saw Emily in the crowd, maybe you should say Hello to her, she was very glad you were fine." Popey thought about this a while, and replied, "And Misha wanted me to stop and see her, she said there'd be work for me. I guess it's the moving work." Lilly shot back quickly, "Yes, she could always depend on you. You're a good worker, Popey." She smiled at him in a way that showed how comfortable she was now that the conversation was on familiar ground.

They stood up together, and started walking back towards the clearing. A steady stream of Hopnegs in all directions told them the crowd had broken up, and Lilly wondered what she missed. Popey honestly didn't care, but he did wonder if the roasted seed vendor was still there. But as they took a turn just before the big clearing, Popey could see that he was out of luck. Besides, his sister might have something just as good at home.

As they rounded the next bend along a carefully worn path, Lilly's house came into view. It was a decent sized tree, not as big as Rouger's but certainly worth noting, that had a small door at the base of a root. Lilly took a large set of keys from her belt, clanked them around until she found the right one, and creaked open the door. Popey still was hungry, but he remembered something important:

"I told Misha I would see her. I'd like to do that before I get all settled and stuff." The force of this pronouncement scared Lilly slightly, but it was best to not keep Misha waiting. "Sure, I'll just get dinner on. Back soon?" "Oh, yeah, I'll be back soon."

Misha lived in a tree just a few steps from Lilly, so it was no time before Popey reached her door and knocked. "Come in, child, come in!" said a voice that nearly opened the door itself, and Popey entered the small root burrow.

Inside, a comfortable fire lighted the dark and musty hollow. The flickers of light played off of oak panels carved by hand into a shape something between a drawing room and a cookie jar. Misha sat on a carved hickory chair with cloth padding on it, and motioned Popey in. "Please, sit!" She motioned to another chair across from her. "Would you like some tea?" Popey declined the tea, but sat in the chair gently. It was dangerously comfortable, and he sank up to his eyeballs in it.

"Child, how are you? You aren't still in shock, are you? Nasty thing, but if anyone could get out, you could."
"Uh, I'm fine, Misha, thank you for having me over. You're very kind."
"Are you sure you are fine, child? Those 'episodes' at the clearing were not like you at all."
Popey simple stared at her. Misha continued:
"Well, I see you aren't interested in apologizing."
"There are other kinds of magic, aren't there!" The determination had built in him again, suddenly.

"Yes, child, there are. But what do you know of them?"
"That they are!" Popey was not giving up.
"Yes, there are other kinds, but we do not have them."
"But you yourself said… you said that the magic of the Demon is broken by looking!"
"Perhaps it is. But you saw it, did it stop?"
"No.… It… didn't." Popey was losing his determination again.
"That is why we must move, child. We have no magic against this."
"But what about the grove? They haven't come here!"
"They will, child. There is more in The Book than what we talk about. It is very clear that when the Giants build homes we have to leave the area. They will take all of our magic sooner or later."

Popey hadn't considered that he wasn't being told everything. Still, there was something terribly wrong with the whole situation. Something could be done, somehow, somewhere.

"Child, please remember that none of us like the idea, either. And think of how this can help you regain your station in life. There is much work to be done, more than Rouger or myself or any of the others can do. You can work hard. We can pay you well. You will be taken care of."

It all became clear to Popey in an instant. Misha was kind, and always looked after them. But she wasn't going to talk to him in public about this arrangement, since that would look bad. Her heart was warm, but it was cooled by her place in the world. Popey didn't know how to feel about this act of charity. In the end, all he could mutter was a thin, "Thank you, Misha, I really appreciate it." Once again, being alive did not matter as much as having a proper position in the world.

The conversation had stopped cold, and between the chair and the flickering fire Popey found himself becoming very sleepy. Misha noticed this, and said from the edge of her seat, "Child, you look tired. You have had a long day. Are you staying with your sister tonight?" Popey's head slumbered over in a gentle roll, and once again something odd came from his mouth: "Tell me about other kinds of magic, Misha. Tell me all the different kinds you know of."

Misha was not used to questions like this, especially not from Popey. It hit her like a slap in the face, the kind that threatens more if an answer is not produced and produced soon. It seemed like it was worth answering, if for no reason than she was an old woman with some ancient knowledge that had to be passed on sometime. Why not now, with the security of this grove wrapped around them all, before the big move?

"Very well, child. There are many kinds of magic, but I am afraid that most of them have been lost. We did not have writing before we learned it from the Giants, and all that we had was passed down in the way I am passing it on now. So many of us were killed when the Giants first arrived, and we were not aware of the danger enough to prepare. We lost a lot of our magic in the hearts and minds of those who perished in these terrible times. So our elders have since studied the magic of the Giants to see what they had, that we might survive.

"They learned about power and status, and they learned about the magic of ownership. But most importantly, they learned that writing was the most powerful magic there is. That is why we guard The Book so carefully and only the most powerful learn to read it.

"The sayings that they wrote down guide us to this day. They are mostly made up of the magic we learned from the Giants. But there was a time when our own magic ruled our lives, and we lived by ourselves. We were often vulnerable, but it did have its useful teachings about how the cycles of the world worked."

Popey felt a cold feeling in his guts, one that threatened to quench the fire he had felt all day. "So there is other magic, but we have all forgotten it?" "My child, it is weak magic, simple things that come from nature. It has so little power it is not important. The Giants nearly killed us all before we stopped relying on it."

Popey drank this all in, but could say nothing. The world had seemed upside down since this morning, but Misha suddenly righted it. He felt his eyelids droop into his lap at the thought. Misha saw him falling asleep, and wondered if her speech wasn't wasted after all. "Child, you need to go home and get some sleep. Tomorrow is a big day, as we will prepare to move. Come, let me help you to the door."

Popey was able to drag himself up, thank Misha for her kindness, and shuffle over to Lilly's house. He knocked ever so gently on the door, and was led directly to the table. After a delicious grass seed stew, he had no time at all for dessert or conversation or even the slightest hint of social grace. He barely made it to the guest bed and fell asleep, in his pajamas the whole time. Lilly wrapped him with a blanket and smiled as tucking in her son rather than her brother. She had been worried about him, but to see him finally rest gave her hope that he would really be fine, after all.

CHAPTER 3:
ACTING SIMPLY

The night brought little sleep to Popey. Just like he woke up, he went to bed tossing and turning and fighting off what seemed like dreams in vain. This time, at least, he really was dreaming. But that didn't help him get the rest he needed. Despite falling asleep before the sun had gone down, his restless sleep kept him in bed much longer than he planned. He nearly slept through the dawn, which he was hoping to greet again.

When sleepiness dropped away from him, Popey saw a thin note of light leaking under the curtains. He sprang himself up with a loud push off his bed and a yank of the drapes to see how late it really was. It was still nighttime, though the sun was beginning to chase the stars away. As Popey settled back in relief, he saw the deep purples and gentle lavenders that matched the curtains so well, Lilly's favorite colors. He smiled as they were giving way to fingers of orange and red. Holding his own fingers up to the light, he wondered what Lilly would think.

"Popey, is that you?" came a gentle voice tapping the door. Popey felt himself turn to it as if his head was on a string, and he stared for a hard minute. He had done all this before. But he had not spent the night in his sister's new house previously. Was this a dream? It was, before, but not now. "Popey?" He had been staring at the door for a long time in a strange kind of terror, afraid of nothing important – but still afraid. "Yes, Lilly, I'm awake."

The door creaked open, and the feeling of dread sprinkled around Popey as though it had popped. He smiled at his sister, who had obviously wakened recently herself. Her small oil lamp suddenly filled his room with light, and he cringed away from it slightly. "Popey, I had to check on you. You fell asleep awfully hard, but had such a fitful night." The worry was tight on her face that was otherwise droopy with sleep. But this was what Popey expected. He smiled back at her, "There's nothing wrong with me that getting an early start won't fix. You know me, Lilly, if I can keep moving I'll be fine."

Lilly smiled at an old familiar feeling that was her first comfort in quite a few hours. She did not like the terrible noises she heard from Popey's room all night. He obviously was in some kind of shock still, and who could blame him? What he had been through was something that no one else could have gone through as cheerfully as he had.

"Sis, I'm going outside. I think it's time I feel some cool air hitting my face." Popey grinned eagerly at Lilly, which made her feel as though everything was suddenly fine. She even forgot about the big move that was coming up, and all the other problems involved in keeping her business running through it all. Her brother looked like his old self again, and that was all she cared about.

"You go on, I'll get breakfast on." And with that Lilly happily turned to the task at hand, forgetting about the bigger problems. That would all come later, but first there had to be breakfast. A big breakfast that could make anyone carefree and fortify them to face their troubles with new strength. Yes, that's what was needed here at the River Flats. Lilly told herself over and over how important her work was.

Popey, meanwhile, found himself drawn to the growing fingers of orange like a moth to a flame. He stepped out the small door at the base of the tree and into the damp morning air, stretching himself out to watch the dawn. This was in his dream, this part right here, and it was a good dream. The orange and red slowly lit up what was left of the field, the tall cordgrass shimmering in the light as if greeting it. A wood duck chirped his hello, brave in the color and light. When he became aware of being spotted, he took flight ahead and away. As his wings beat the air in time to his whistle, he stirred up the grass-wet smell rising slowly in the warmth. The orange and now yellow sun wrapped around and enveloped Popey as if hugging a long lost friend.

As gorgeous as this was, Popey still felt strangely out of sorts. Normally, the feeling that the prairie grass could hide him entirely was a great comfort, as it dazzled back and forth through the growing orange light. But now, it made him feel as though he were very small. Or perhaps the world seemed very big. It was hard to tell which. This was never a concern before, but it seemed very real with the arrival of the Giants and their Demons. Yet however large the world was, they obviously could travel it with ease, as if it were small to them.

None of this made sense, not in Popey's head. The only thing he was sure of was that the smell of acorn porridge coming under the door was a very good thing indeed. The rest of it, well, he might form opinions about in more detail later.

Finishing up his breakfast calmly, he could see his sister eagerly waiting for more signs that he was back to being his old self. He wanted to ask her about his dreams, but realized that Lilly could never be happy worrying about her brother's dreams. He decided that he needed to go along, just like he usually did. He loved her too much not to play his role well, he thought, even though it caused him grief that he couldn't confide in her.

"That was great, it really was, Lilly." Popey sincerely told her, "That should keep me going through what promises to be a big day... a really busy day, that is!" Lilly smiled back, "Glad you like it, Bro." Popey finished cleaning up his place and was drying the pan Lilly had used so he could hang it back up. "Lilly, I have to get off to visit Emily, I said her I'd see her yesterday! And I'd like to go and ah... finish up some of what Misha and I were talking about last night." Lilly sank a little at the thought of moving, but she was glad her brother was interested in getting back on track. "Oh, about the work she has for you?" "Ah... yes, the work. Lots of it, I'm sure. Well, I'm off, thanks a lot!"

Popey hung the pan up in its spot and kissed his sister on the cheek. She muttered some faint goodbye, but somehow it was lost in her deeper feelings. As cheerful as Popey was, something seemed wrong to Lilly, a small wrench in her guts that she vowed to not pay a lot of attention to. It had to be wrong, didn't it?

It was his own strange feeling, like having escaped, that warmed Popey like the dawn once he was out the door. It was a feeling he could grow to love, but knew he hated deep down. It was as if everything were coiled up into one big ball that was so tightly wound it might explode any minute. That's what really made him think about Emily, and how relaxed he felt around her.

Popey had been sort of dating Emily, sort of not, for what seemed like a long time now. They were more friends than anything. A lot of the time she said very little, especially about herself. But she always knew just what to say to make him feel happy, and that suited him right now. Too many things were going on right now. The last thing he needed was something more.

He plodded over the floor of the grove to the small burrow at the edge under the big rock where Emily lived. Walking up to the door with great confidence, he knocked loudly. "Who is it?" came the voice inside. "It's just little ol' me!" cried Popey in a familiar song.

The door burst open, and Emily sucked in the air between them and drew Popey into her nearly desperate embrace. "Popey! Oh, thank goodness! Oh!... Popey!" She was sobbing gently by the time Popey even had a chance to look at her. How long had it been, 3 weeks since he had seen her? The snow wasn't gone all that long, and it was that odd warm spell the last time he made it over here. Emily still looked good, still liked that funny light blue and white checked dress of hers with the dark blue cloak around her. And the smell of her brown hair brought back so many good memories.

"I heard you lost your home and no one had seen you and then there was that meeting and I almost got to you before Lilly did and I wanted you to come and stay with me, well, I know you still have family but you know that you can stay with me while..." She was blushing badly as her sentence trailed off, but Popey knew what she meant. Emily just wanted a chance to return some of the favors of all the work Popey had done for her over the years, is all. Besides, she might even love him, he never knew for sure.

"I'm sorry I didn't see you yesterday, but I got real tired after that meeting and barely made it through dinner. I hope you understand, Emily."
"I do, Popey, I'm just glad you made it out."
"Yeah, I am too. You know, I, ah... I lost everything."
"I realize that, Popey. I don't have that much magic either, you know."

20

"Yeah, well, I'm pretty much a Punk now."
"That's allright. You made it out, and that's what counts."
Emily knew what mattered, and that made Popey glad.

"Popey, will you come in? I have breakfast cooking!"
"I already ate, thanks. Lilly took care of me, as usual."
"Oh, I'm sure she takes care of you well, Popey!"

A strange thought crossed Popey's mind, where he compared the women in his life. They all seemed to 'take care of him' in their own ways, yet none of them really took care of everything. It was Lilly he went to in time of crisis, but she couldn't be told how he really felt. Emily was the one he could say anything to, but she rarely let on just what she was thinking herself. They were so different, and yet so important to him. What was the missing thing that could bring them together? This thought came to him as he walked into Emily's cramped dirt home. It floated him above the hard packed floor, as if he wasn't totally there. And it occurred to him that he was the one that separated them, and he was the one that brought them together. He floated there a moment, wondering why anyone had to 'take care of him'.

"Sit over here, Popey, this is the comfortable chair!" Emily nearly squeaked at the sight of him. "Tell me, what was that awful Demon like! How have you been?" Popey sat down gently, still slightly floating and giddy at the realization that so many things were suddenly making sense to him. After he recounted the thumping and rolling and running story yet again, he felt an urge to ask something. That strange voice from the day before, the one that spoke up to Rouger, came out firmly but gently this time.

"Em, I had a dream last night. Maybe you can help me with it."

She'd done this many times before with him, it was what they loved to do. They could talk about dreams long into when it was time to have some new ones. But he'd never been so abrupt – in fact, he was usually a bit shy about the whole thing.

"Of course, Popey, you know I love talking about dreams, what they mean."
"This one was different, though."

"Tell me."
"Allright, I will..."

"I'm standing at the edge of a field, and the sun is either setting or rising – I can't tell which. It's all orange and the air is cool and soft and... well, and I'm about to walk off into the sunlight, when I hear... I hear a voice. I don't know whose voice it is. But it calls my name, and I turn around. I don't want to turn around, but I do. And once I've turned around, I can't look back at the sun and walk to where I was going, I have to find out who was calling me. I just can't go on... ahead once that happens."

Emily sat there a moment, wondering what to say about this. It seemed very straightforward, but Popey's voice was so determined that it seemed like he really wanted to walk off, maybe leave forever. She didn't like that, but hid her feelings out of habit.

"Well, I don't know about the sun, but I do know that names have a lot of power. There's a special magic in your name, and knowing your name gives someone the power to hold your attention no matter what. At least for a while. I mean, well... your name is who you are, in a lot of ways."

Popey thought about this, and decided that, as usual, Emily was right. "So to have power over someone, we need to know their name. Or something... we name it, and we... know something about it and what it is, right?"
"Um, I guess that makes sense. But that wasn't in your dream, was it?"
"In a way, it was. I think that whoever was calling my name didn't really know me, they just knew my name."

Emily wasn't sure about all this. It started out kind of fun, but the conversation had somehow left her longing to back up a bit. "Popey, does this have to do with that awful Demon? Do you think it was calling your name when you were running from it?" Popey had to think about that one a moment, and he let the air out between his teeth before he actually formed words around them, "Nooo, that's sort of... close, but not quite. I'm thinking a moment... I'm not sure, but... Em, do you think that dreams can give you ideas, how to do stuff?"

Emily hadn't considered this idea before, but let a short "Yeah" out as she nodded. Why not? Dreams can tell you a lot about the future, she reasoned, so why not how to handle it as well? But since Popey was clearly thinking about something, she let the words fail a moment and waited for him to continue. It unnerved her when he didn't for a long time. Then, he finally said something, but in a voice that didn't seem like his:

"Em, I'm going to be real busy for a while here. I've got some stuff to do. This could all work out... it could".
"Are you fine, Popey? You're not still all... woozy and stuff?"
"No, no... I feel really good in a way. Look, you don't have to worry about me anymore, allright?"
"I'll always worry about you, you know that."
"I... I don't want you to, though. I really do feel... great!"
"You're so different, now... you don't seem right."
"I'm not different, really, I'm just seeing things better than I used to, is all."
"What does that mean?" The conversation was drifting away from her again, and that made her very uncomfortable.
"It means that I have ideas about things, and I don't just want to do what I'm told and so on. That's all."
"Well, that seems good enough."

There was a long pause that stood between them for what seemed like forever. Popey realized he was just trying to find a way to get away and move forward with the idea percolating in his mind. So he stood up to make his intentions known. "Well, Em, it's been a lot of fun, and I do appreciate your help a lot, but things are going to get pretty busy around here." Emily couldn't hide her disappointment that he was leaving, but tried not to talk about it. "Oh, Popey, you're welcome anytime here. You know that. I love to know what you're thinking."

And with that, Popey was goodbye and out the door and off to somewhere but he wasn't sure. Who could he talk to about his idea? He kept his feet moving, but they weren't going anywhere he had thought of. And then the idea crossed his mind – Rodele, yes Rod would be a good person to talk about this stuff. He's so kind and he's young enough to work this out without getting some hard opinion on it, Rod is a good idea.

Rodele lived in the next field over, on the other side of the grove. The Demon hadn't been through there yet, but everyone assumed it was a matter of time. In fact, as Popey made his way over to the warm sunlight and tall grasses that framed it, he could see the Demon puffing away at a far corner of the field. It was only a matter of time.

Popey found the small burrow entrance with the rock roof and slit rain gutter. He called out, "Helloo!" to see if Rod was there, and shortly heard a scurry inside. "Come in!" went the scurry, and Popey followed it into the burrow, dark and cold as it was.

Rodele had been packing, and all around him were sacks tied up with string. "Popey, my friend, what a pleasant surprise. Yes, I'm just getting ready to move like all the others. Sad, this is." It seemed as though there were an awful lot of sacks, and Popey could swear that some were filled with rocks. "Yes, Rod, it is sad. That's why I've been trying to think of a reason we don't have to do it, another way... around the problem".

Rod perked up a moment at this, and motioned for Popey to sit in the one chair that remained out on the hard-packed dirt floor. As he did this, Rod hovered a moment looking for a place to park himself. Finding none, he kicked a sack a few times until it was about the size and shape of his backside, and settled into it. "So what did you have in mind, Popey?"

"Well, this sort of came to me in a dream."
"Sort of?"
"Um, it did. An idea like it... as I thought about the dream, then it pretty much came to me."
"Allright, so the basic idea was there but you had to think about it some."
"Yes, Rod, that's it. Precisely. I'm... ah, new at being clever."
Rod smiled so hard at that last remark that he had trouble talking.
"Popey, dear friend, tell me your idea. I assure you that you are just as clever as you need to be."

Popey smiled back, happy to be heard finally.

Chapter 4:
Perfect Trust

"Well, Rod, it starts like this. See, I remembered something from when I was running from... that thing out there. It breathes just like we do. I heard it, I think I even felt it. It sucks in air in the front and blasts out smoke at the top."

Rodele looked at him for a moment, not understanding at all what Popey was going on about. His face drooped a little when he thought he might be wasting his time after all. "I'm afraid I can't see where you are going, Popey. So it breathes? Wha... What does that matter?"

Popey cleared his throat. "If it breathes we can stop it from breathing and kill it. Suffocate it. You know... like the way the grasshopper mouse traps work, by stuffing grass into it. It wouldn't breathe unless it had to, and if we can stop it... then, well..."

He trailed off, letting his words follow Rodele's head to the floor. This was harder than he thought. "I know, it'll be hard to get enough people up there to stuff enough in, but that's the secret of it all, getting everyone working together."

Rodele finally looked right at Popey, wondering if there was more to this story. "Yes, and how do you propose to do that?" Popey smiled just a little, "That's where my dream comes in. If we name that Demon, even just the name we have for it, we can tell everyone that it's nothing to be afraid of. It won't have as much magic if we can tell them that 'this is a Thumper and we can get it by stuffing grass into it'. Once we let people know that we understand it, and call the thing by name, it loses a lot of its magic."

Rodele's head turned skeptically, but he returned Popey's smile. "So you think we can stop this whole thing, and not move, right? Is that your plan?" Popey nodded, and Rodele suddenly leaned back and relaxed and looked much more comfortable. "Go on, please... go on."

"Well, I think we can get this, or at least try, if we all... get together. I just didn't know how to break some of the magic, until my dream is all. Does this make sense? I mean, I want to try to get this together a bit before we can go and tell Rouger that maybe we don't have to move."

"Rouger is an idiot," Rodele answered flatly. "He's completely worthless. He doesn't do anything – Misha does all the work." The last part didn't surprise Popey, really, but the spitting tone of Rodele's speech caught him off guard – "But... you don't really mean he's an idiot, do you?" "Yes, I do. All he does is pull stuff out of The Book and tell us what it says. You know how he got to be so rich?" Popey shook his head, still bewildered. "Popey, he's rich because he has other people do all the work for him. This frees his time to make deals, both among us and with the Travelers. If it weren't for Misha, he'd have nothing."

Popey thought about this a second, but knew what to say back. "Yes, but he can read! As long as he has The Book, he has all the wisdom of... years at his hands!" Rodele sneered in a way that looked a bit too violent for Popey's liking. "Read? That's what he's good for, to read? I can read too, you know! It's not that hard! I could be the leader, you know!"

The last sentence made Popey stop a moment. Could Rod do a better job than Rouger, the old fop who had been so terribly mean to him, and wouldn't listen to him at all? Certainly, Rouger was awfully quick to leave, awfully quick to run away.

Popey's eyes darted around, hoping to find something to say. Nothing came to him, nothing seemed like the answer among the sacks of Rodele's possessions stacked everywhere. And during that time, his guard was down, slightly, and that strange feeling bubbled back into his head. He wasn't quite sure why he spoke like he did:

"Rod, could you lead the charge against that thing? Let's call it a Thumper, can we get everyone together around that?"

Rodele's grin folded back into his face for a moment at how Popey ignored the blurting out of his real intentions. But it spread out again when he understood that Popey was committing himself to this one great act, his one real shot at proving he could lead. This was his day. He would have to use all of his skill, but he could do it.

"Popey, my friend, I would be honored to lead this. I never wanted to leave this beautiful spot on the River Flats, and I take it you never did either, right? Well, the time has come for us to act. Can you round up all of your friends, those whom you can trust, and get them to come here for a meeting in, say," he held his hand to the window, "one handspan of sun?" "Certainly, Rod, I can round up a few people for a mission like this. Quite a few, I think. I don't think anyone wants to run away."

Rodele got a solemn look on his face, and lowered his voice as if someone was suddenly listening, "And make sure you do this in secret, as much as you can. No one is to know more than they need to, understood?"

Popey looked at him as if his face were chiseled from stone. "Rod, I know your intentions. Do not worry. We can do this. Count on me." And with that, Popey went out of the cluttered burrow to find some friends he knew he could count on.

He went far and wide through the grove and the edge of the field, and all through the River Flats to find some of the Hopnegs he knew he could count on. Most were friends, a few were people he'd worked with, and some others were more distant than that. Though not all of the faces were familiar to him, all of these faces were ones he had seen twist or recoil or even scowl when Rouger announced it was time to move. Popey had a gift for noticing things like that, and he was happy to put it to use.

At the end of his corkscrew windings through the whole community, he paused for a moment at the door of Misha's house. It was nearly lunchtime; perhaps she was in resting for a moment before getting back to the harsh work of organizing and arranging and all the other things that fell to her. Popey wanted to stop and see her before this project filled his mind so completely that it pushed that thought out. But here he was. A knock was all it took.

He rapped at her door with a conviction like he knew what he wanted. But when the voice answered, "Come in" with the force of Misha behind it, the determination suddenly fell away. After all, it was the assault on the... Thumper?... that he wanted to tell her about, and that was now a secret. Besides, he always felt a bit small and shy when he was around her.

But then Popey remembered the other part, the little bit how to work the magic once you think you've found it. That was what still eluded him. Once you have the power, what can you do with it? He would need Misha's help, for although she never wielded power on her own it was obvious to everyone she had some. And her sense of magic and how it works was what he needed now.

"Hello, Misha, might I see you for a moment?"
"Yes, my child, come in, sit down. I was just settling in for... a little meal. Would you care to join me?"
"No, Misha, thank you very much." His determination was building again.
"The work on the move will begin tomorrow, we have nearly planned out all the awful details"
"Thank you, but that's not what I wanted to ask you. I was interested in other kinds of magic again... what we were talking about before I got sleepy."

Misha put down her Dandelion milk and turned her head as if straining to understand Popey. But the smile on her face showed that she heard every word – that it wasn't the words that escaped her, but the person saying them.

"Go on, child."
"Well, I really know what you mean now that there are other kinds. But I don't really know that they are all weak."
"No, child, I suppose some must be strong. But we do not know what magic there is that summons Demons like we have seen."
"We've worked so hard to... to learn about this, and write it down, but the Giants still have much stronger magic than we do. Or so we think."
"Dear child, I am sure they still have stronger magic than we do. And perhaps we can learn about it. But we have been so busy trying

to survive and stay ahead of them that we have not learned these things."

Once again, Popey realized that he had not considered the situation completely. There was more to it than his elders were letting on. "Misha, I think we need to try things. You know, see what we can do. I really think that... I always learn by trying things out. I..."

With that, he trailed off. Misha was clearly not following him as her brow wrinkled tightly, as if to close the gap between them.

"Dear child, I can see you have an interest in some of the mysterious ways of the world. Now that you are grown, perhaps you can do more than lift heavy loads for us all. Would you like to be my student when we are done with the moving?"

Popey hadn't thought about that. He was so busy trying to ask about his plan without revealing it that he hadn't considered the larger future. He felt tired again, realizing that his cleverness and urge to do something left him far too busy worrying about what was around him to see the bigger picture.

"Um, Misha, yes, I would like that very much. I... ah, I think that we have a lot to learn and I would like to be... I would like that, yes. Thank you!"

Misha's face rebounded quickly, and started to glow softly. This was what she really wanted all along, a student like Popey to whom she could pass on what she knew. And in this instant, Popey realized that he wasn't the only one who was blinded by his cleverness. All the Hopnegs were so very busy that they could only learn what stood in front of their small frames before they passed through it – and then left it in their wake. More importantly, Misha understood this.

"Dear child, I can see you have learned much already. You have taught yourself how to pay attention and ask questions. You understand there is more to it than most of us see. But I can teach you more, much more."
"You can teach me to use a different magic?"

"I can teach you to find it on your own. Perhaps you can make it powerful, dear child. That would be up to you."

Popey sank into his chair slowly, as if compressing the springs that would lift him back out of it. It was time to go. Misha didn't really answer his questions, but he didn't ask them. There were other questions anyways, ones he hadn't thought of yet.

"Misha, I have some other work to do. Thank you again. I'd really like to be your student. That would be... great, really. Thank you."

"Dear child, we are all so busy. I know you have much to do, we all do. It is the times we live in." She sighed heavily at the last comment.

Popey stood up, and thanked Misha for what seemed like the hundredth time, and showed himself to the door. As it clicked behind him, the warming air of the midday jolted him awake again, and he realized that the time to gather over at Rodele's house was upon him. It was time to go into action. He sprinted over to the edge of the grove and saw a small crowd had gathered out in the field. They were mostly younger, his friends and colleagues, and they were chatting up a noisy cloud of dirt and sound. As he approached the small hill that marked Rodele's house, he saw his friend steeling himself to address the crowd.

"Popey, there you are! I was, ah... I started to think you wouldn't be here. I've thought about this some, and what we need here is leadership. You wouldn't mind if I took command here, since I have some experience in this, would you?"

Popey shrugged gently, and muttered, "No, no, go ahead." And with that, Rodele strode up to the top of his house with determination, stood there, and waved for silence. He quickly got it.

"Friends, thank you for coming here today." Rodele's voice boomed over the crowd, holding them still by its force. "This is a grave time at the River Flats. But most importantly, it is time to make some decisions. We have to decide if we are going to cringe before this challenge, as some would have us do, and run away like so many grasshopper mice. Or, are we going to stand up and fight, take our destiny into our hands?!"

He paused a moment to allow the crowd to murmur its surprise. He continued without shushing them:

"That is the choice we have, and it is our choice. There are those who call themselves 'leaders' who will tell you that we do not have a choice, but don't you believe them! True leaders are those who give the people what they want, who find a way no matter how clever they have to be, to give you what it is that you need. And tell the truth, friends, do any of you actually want to leave here? Do any of you really want to pack all of your things and scurry off like you had tails?"

The murmurs of the crowd formed themselves into a splatter of "No!"s, which gathered together into a chant of "No! No! We won't go!" Popey looked back over the crowd and saw that one Hopneg, someone he knew was another friend of Rodele's, was leading the cheers and getting the crowd organized. Popey smiled at the thought of everyone working together, even if it was only to shout. For the first time, he really thought this might actually work. Rodele held his arms out to silence the crowd, and in that one wide swipe they sucked in their chant in unison.

Rod continued. "Ever since this terrible Demon appeared, I have labored to develop a plan. I stayed up late into the night thinking of things we could do. While others were packing, I focused myself on how we could stay here, how we could get that Demon. And when I finally collapsed in exhaustion, it came to me in a dream. The idea, the way, the plan that will allow us all to stay in the River Flats. But you have to all be with me! United, we can do it! Are you with me?!"

The crowd yelled out "Yes!" as if one. Popey was excited, but wondered where this was going. It wasn't quite as he thought it would be. His eyes darted around from one face to the next, trying to read them.

"My research has informed me that this thing is what we call a 'Vromba'. It is a terrible beast, for sure, but it breathes and eats just as we do. It is vulnerable! There is no need to run from it, when we can destroy it!"

At this the crowd cheered and whistled not as a mob but as individual people overjoyed that they were finally getting an explanation.

"A Vromba can be brought down by the same cleverness that we Hopnegs use to stifle the dreaded grasshopper mice. Yes, citizens, we are not mice ourselves – and we know what to do with Vrombas like we know what to do with mice!"

Popey felt himself flinch at the word "citizens". His dream was turning into something of a nightmare. But the goal was still important, and he would swallow that turn in his guts if it meant that they could stay.

"What we must do is gather grasses, as much as we can carry, as if we were building a Giant suffocating trap. And when the Vromba has paused for a moment, as it will do soon, we must climb up to its mouth and stuff them all in. It will gasp, and die, if we can only get enough brave citizens up there to take on this noble task. I will lead us all, if you will but follow and claim your land, your home, and your destiny. Who is with me?!"

At this, a great cheer rose from the crowd, a wild bubbling excitement that showed that they would indeed have enough men to accomplish the task. Popey was glad it was all working out, but wondered why Rodele had to twist the story so much to get them to this point. Glancing around, he saw the crowd dispersing slowly to pick over the field and collect hunks of dried grass. The frenzied activity and shouting was interrupted only by the shout of Rodele, "Gather all you can, and we will march to the far field and prepare for victory!"

With that, Rodele leapt from his perch and started tramping through the grove to the other field. Behind him was a bobbing mass of grass and thatch that twittered with excitement, falling into line and following their leader as if off to war. Popey grabbed a hunk of grass as well, but he could feel that he was not as interested in this trip as his comrades. His place was to the rear of the long line, watching the procession move in front of him.

After a short while, they reached the other field. The bright sun blinded everyone briefly, so the armfuls of grass were raised to shield the eyes of each of the warriors. And once they got used to the light, there it stood. Down by the road, near the great sign, puffing slightly but not moving. The Demon, what ever you call it, was indeed idle. It was time to strike.

Rodele motioned with his arm, unfettered by grass tufts, and told his band, "Move along the grove quickly but without running. Then, when we are near it at the far end, we wait until we are all together, and then run to it. Climb the black part near the shiny wall, and from there scale the sides. I will go up first and bring a rope. You will see the mouth when we are there, and I will give the order when it is time. Forward!"

Rodele had obviously taken some time to know his enemy. But Popey was still wary of the operation, in part because the more time he had to reflect on what had just happened, the more it scared him. He was content to bring up the rear, not sure of each footstep. The group gradually got into position at the edge of the grove, and Rodele asked who had ropes. A few hands were raised, and Rodele put them in front. Then, after a long breath, came the call.

"For our home! Come on!"

Shouts of "Our home!" were raised as the raft of grass tufts moved briskly across the flat field of dirt. This section had been well pounded by the Demon, and the charge was easy and swift. As they got behind the steel wall, the noise was deafening but steady. Popey found his heart pounding in a way that was both frightening and exciting at the same time.

No one could hear anything, so what cries they made as they scaled went unheard. Rodele went up first, grabbing the knobs of the black section easily and getting his feet at the top of it. After that, it was a hard climb for him to the very top, scrambling over tubes and beams until he stood on the yellow roof, shaking and rumbling as the Demon did. The process was tedious, but as this happy band stood there they realized they were not being hurt. The Demon could not hurt them after all! This was going to work!

Once on top, Rodele sent down his line, which was quickly grabbed by another Hopneg with a rope around his shoulders. Soon, another joined him and another, and then lines were dropped all along the yellow body and strange limbs. It was a short time before they were all up there, losing only a small amount of their load as they went.

Popey was once again at the end, and he found it remarkably easy to scale the rope. His blood was boiling from fear and a sense of pending triumph, and in front of him all he could see was victory. The foul smoke, thicker at the top, only made him laugh at the thought of quenching it forever.

When he finally heaved himself over the top, he saw his comrades gathering by the strange round disk that was greedily sucking in air. Rodele motioned to it, and appeared to call a charge, but no one heard him in the deafening rumble. But they all knew what to do. The rush of Hopnegs over to the thing had the look of an epic painting, a moment they would all remember forever. They were slaying the Demon!

The bales of grass were thrown heavily into the sucking disk, and very quickly, it happened. The noise became uneven, the quaking rattle more violent. Rodele motioned everyone away, and they all slid down the ropes as quickly as they could in fear of retribution. Popey felt the great sense of victory draining from him as he hoped to escape only with his life, once again. When the ropes were cleared, and they were yanked off their moorings at the top, the scene collapsed into chaos. Some of them jumped, some climbed down, but they all moved as quickly as they could to escape the wrath of this Demon. And just as Popey jumped to the ground, it happened.

Nothing.

It was silent, unwavering, not puffing or quaking. It was dead. They had done it! They had slain the Demon!

Popey could not believe how well it all worked. Just a quick moment and it was all done, all right. Victory was theirs! They would not have to move, they would not have to go!

All that remained was a quick sprint back to the grove before the Giants showed up to see what happened to their magic, and they would all be safe and secure. And when the band got to the grove, a great cheer went up for the leader who had showed them the way, the great Rodele!

Chapter 5:
Shameless

The sizzle of victory in Popey's blood was suddenly thrown into the sharp twist in his guts, and came back sharp and nasty. Something told him that this was not the end of an episode, but the beginning of something else.

It was the way the crowd lifted Rodele up with their voices, and then their arms that gave Popey this feeling. He was the one that thought this idea up, and there he was in the back, unnoticed. As Rodele bounced along the boiling crowd, lifted up and down by the chant of "Our Home! Our Home!" Popey fell back a little further. He couldn't describe the feeling that something was stolen from him. Jealousy? Insult? Whatever the feeling was, it made him feel so much smaller. So much smaller than the now towering, grinning figure of Rodele, lifted in triumph.

The band continued into the grove, gradually seeking the safety of the woods, as they should. Popey held back, wondering what to make of it all. He stood at the edge of the grove, one side in sunlight and the other in darkness, staring at the ground as if it would tell him the answer. As he looked down at his pajamas, now filthy beyond description, he saw the light divide him in half. Both parts were Popey, but each had its calling. The sunlight was warm and refreshing, the shade of the grove cool and safe. And in this way, the ground finally gave him his answer.

His eyes lifted and darted quickly to survey the scene. Rodele and his band had gone off far enough that the air was nearly still and quiet. The Demon stood there, dead. But what was it? There were fenceposts between where he stood and the Demon, he could sneak up for a closer look. And so he did.

Slowly at first, then quickly with a jumping run he dashed for the posts and then from one to the next. He would learn what this particular thing was. He would make sure it didn't harm them ever again. This was the thing that changed him, this was the Demon that stole everything from him. He had to know what it was, had to know it was really dead.

He quickly made his way to the post nearest the carcass. It was silent, yet so large that Popey still feared it. He slid one eye past the frame of the post to peer quietly at the yellow mass that glinted sunlight so strong it hurt. Popey's heart pounded in a way that made it hard to focus, one eye at a time, and the harsh smell of the fencepost bottom painted his throat with a dry, sickly feeling.

Just then, he spotted something new. Four large Boot Mountains had arrived on the scene. Popey dashed his head back behind the post to avoid being spotted, and listened to what the enormous boots had to say.

"Is she out of gas, there? I told you not to let her run over lunch."
"It's a diesel, they're better on idle. And she's got half a tank."
"What else coulda gone wrong with her?"
"Oh, I see what we got here. The air filter's full up."
"Wouldja look at that. That looks like the work of Prairie Gnomes, doncha know!"
"Ah, Geez, Bob. It was the wind picked up this mess, is all."
"No, this is the sorta thing my Nana told me about. Prairie Gnomes don't like havin' their homes wrecked and all. They do this stuff."
"Yeah, well, your Grandma was a bit different, you know."
"No, she knew about this kind of stuff. Said she saw them, out in the fields. They don't like living where there's people, for some reason. They like to be out by themselves, so no one hardly sees 'em."
"Well, whatever. That'll do her. Prairie Gnomes or not, she's good to go."

And with that, there was a strange whirring noise and a whoosh and a roar and suddenly – it was back! The terrible rumble shook the earth, the Demon was alive again! As Popey's eyes grew so large they nearly fell to the ground, the acrid smoke swept over him in a thick, greasy cloud. He could hardly breathe, but if he coughed, he feared he might be seen. He had to get out, now, and quickly. But how?

He held his hand to his mouth to shield it from the nasty air as he looked around the post ever so carefully. The rumble was louder and shook the earth even more, and it was moving off forward. The Boot Mountains were nowhere to be seen, so it was time to run with his last lungfull of air. 'I can make it to the grove', he thought, 'I can do this, I can get to safety, I can!'

He got to the end of the fencepost row and turned into the grove. The moment he felt the shade fall on his face he collapsed. 'The air is clean here', he thought, and lay there a while gasping and flopping in a raw panic. 'I am safe, for now. But it is alive! The Demon wasn't killed, it is alive! I must warn the others.' But it was some time before he could gather his strength to get up and continue onward to find the rest of his people. His determination was gone, defeated by panic and failure and a lack of air. He lay on his back, not moving except to heave his chest in a desperate search for breath.

When he finally felt he could get up, he found that he was deeply embarrassed by his plan's failure. He wanted to run away and hide, and might have had he not remembered that Rodele had taken all the credit. Surely, he would be subject to all the blame as well. Popey smiled a sickly kind of smile, a smirk that slid across his mouth for just a moment before he realized that there was real danger. The others must know. He must warn everyone. The Demon was alive!

He stumbled up on all fours, and found his feet wobbly but workable. He started in a slow trot through the thick understory of the grove, making a path where there was none. In a few plodding moments, he heard the voices of a crowd in the distance and took his bearings from that. The whole community had gathered, no doubt to celebrate the victory they didn't know was not to be had. Popey picked up speed in a paced, deliberate run.

But as he got closer, the voices didn't sound happy. They weren't celebrating. They sounded angry and sharp, like a terrible fight was going on. As he rounded the last small stand of saplings before the clearing, it was Rodele's voice he heard first:

"You're not fit to be the leader! You wanted to run away! We didn't have to run away, we just needed a leader who was clever and brave and had the power to stand up to these Giants and their Demons!"

There was a cheering roar at the end of this speech, followed shortly by a series of boos and shouts of "No!" that fought for volume despite being meek and confused. As Popey found the clearing in his sight, he could see the huge crowd, disorganized and busy. At the front of this crowd, Rodele was angrily pointing at Rouger with bulging eyes and a waving finger. Rouger merely stood there, a deep red color of embarrassment and fear and anger all at once. He waved to silence the crowd, and nearly got their attention when Popey saw his chance:

"The Demon! It's alive! It's back to life again! I saw it! Look!"

The part of the crowd nearest the field scampered over to where Popey was pointing. A huge gasp swept over them, and at least one person fainted. Shouts of "The Demon!" and "I knew it!" were heard. It was utter pandemonium. Popey stood there at the back catching his breath, feeling utterly drained at the sight. All he wanted was for everyone to work together to solve this problem, and now they were torn apart.

Rodele started to cringe into a much smaller, heavier shape at this scene, and attempted to slip away from the front of the crowd. Rouger grabbed him by the arm as his anger reached out to gather the situation back to his control. With his other arm waving, he bellowed out:

"Silence! Citizens, please, SILENCE!"

The crowd grew meek as the situation got away from them. They quieted easily and suddenly. They wanted to know more. Rouger did, too, and swung his arm around to point to Popey. "Tell me what you know!"

Popey felt a great strength rise in him, now that he was addressed directly. All he ever wanted to do was tell Rouger what he knew, what he saw. Finally, in this disaster, he was given his chance. He wasn't ashamed at all to relish the moment:

"I saw the Giants go to the Demon, and they knew how to take the grass out of its mouth. They also knew how to bring it back to life. I think there were two of them. One of them knew about Hopnegs and saw this as something that we could have done."

The last statement set off a gasp through the crowd, and put a sickly half-smile on Rouger' face. He turned on Rodele quickly, letting go of his arm by way of throwing him to the ground. "You see what you have done! You could have been seen! They know about us! If they had seen you, they would have stopped at nothing to kill us all!" he spat.

Rodele was thin and pale, and cowered in the dirt as though he was about to be killed. "I... I didn't know... I'm sorry, it was a clever idea..." Popey saw Lilly and Misha coming towards him, fighting their way through the crowd. This emboldened him even more, and he spoke up with a force that he did not know was ever inside him:

"This was my idea. I came up with the plan. You have no one to blame but me."

Lilly stopped some distance in front of Popey, and covered her face with her hands. Misha turned her head as if to understand him better, as she had done before, her face ashen white and suddenly much older looking. Rodele scampered off into the crowd, unseen. Rouger stopped bellowing and realized that the situation he thought was coming back into his control was still chaotic and dangerous. "Please explain yourself, young man. Tell us what you... had in mind." Rouger's voice was even and calm, but wavered slightly at the end.

"That Demon took everything from me, except for my life. But it also taught me that there are other kinds of magic, other kinds of power. We are all afraid of the Giants, we fear them. And that is why we have no magic against them. Don't you see? Fear is the opposite of magic, being afraid is the same as having no magic. We are all so busy, all the time, because if we took a moment to stop it we'd realize how terribly afraid we all are."

41

Rouger felt the situation moving even further from his grasp. He spoke up quickly and pointedly: "Young man, we are afraid because they nearly killed us all. If that is not a reason to fear them, what is? That is why The Book was written. So that we may understand their ways and live despite them!"

Popey felt a rising warmth at being addressed directly by Rouger, in front of everyone. It wasn't the anger of the day before, but something much better. He spoke plainly and calmly from deep in his guts:

"The Book says how we should be just like the Giants. We want to be just like them because we fear them. It's the circle of fear that keeps us from realizing the real magic that is around us, within us, all of us, together. But we can't have the same magic they do if we want it only out of fear!"

He was losing the crowd now; they were murmuring gently. Rouger felt this, but had no idea what to do. Only Misha saw where this was going, and her face beamed with an inner radiance that loosened her wrinkles and sparkled her eyes. Lilly saw this in her friend, and looked puzzled and awestruck. Something was happening. Popey took a deep breath as he saw them, and the cool air filled his lungs with an even tighter determination than before. He was right. About what, he wasn't sure. But Rouger still had his control of the situation. He spoke evenly and carefully.

"Young man, leaving your little 'plan' behind us as a tragic failure, do you not realize that The Book is right, and we must leave this place? Do you not understand how the wisdom of those who wrote The Book is still, after all your machinations, the only way to go?"

Popey fumbled. In a strange way, he suddenly stopped caring. Rouger was talking at one level, and he was at another. They would never see eye to eye on this, never. He had The Book, and Popey had nothing – nothing but this strange feeling:

"You may well be right. We enjoyed many happy years here, and they may be over. But we squandered our time. We spent all this time accumulating what we though was real magic, but I don't think it is. I lost all of what I had gathered in one instant, and yet I'm still alive. I know there is more magic than the few things I lost. There must be. That's all."

Rouger had a puzzled expression, but Misha still beamed at him. She nodded gently after his last speech, and some in the crowd were staring more at her than Popey – and none more than Lilly. What was he talking about? Rouger prodded him one last time:

"So you, the plotter of this little 'plan', you agree that we must move?"
"Yes, Rouger, I think you all must move. I do not know if I should go with you."

With this, the crowd that had been silent for too long already started to bubble. Rouger went back to his usual form, "Well, Citizens, it is clear then, is it not, that this unfortunate incident did not end badly nor did it derail our plans to move on. None of us want to move, but we must understand that it is vital. As The Book says, 'The joyous task is the rare task'. We must accept our fate lest we lose everything in these... these foolish schemes."

Somewhere, towards the end of this speech, Lilly finally went up and embraced her brother warmly and unashamedly. "Popey, I don't understand this at all, but I love you. Don't leave us." Misha was at her side, and in the eternity before Lilly let go of Popey said softly, "Dear child, I wanted to teach you what I know, but I understand now that you can teach me. But if you must leave, do it to learn more. And please, send word back."

Popey had once again confused himself. He wasn't sure why he said 'I do not know if I should go with you', but he did. And everyone was taking it like he had made his mind up. Drinking this in, slowly, he saw Emily run up to him. The crowd was breaking up, Rouger was obviously done.

"Popey, oh Popey..." Emily whispered as she wrapped herself around him. "I... ah, liked your speech much better than Rod's". "Thanks, Em, but I didn't hear what he said." Emily let him go to look at him. "It was awful, all full of power and stuff. I thought there might be violence!" Popey saw Lilly nod in agreement. "I'm so glad you learned to follow your dreams, Popey, but will you really leave us?"

Each time this was brought up, Popey was more confused. He didn't realize that the idea shocked them so much that none of his friends or Lilly really knew what to say. They wanted to know more, but he had no more. He didn't really know where that statement came from.

"Em, I don't know. I kind of thought I might have to. But I do want to find out more about... about stuff, you know..." the word magic wasn't working for him. But another word wasn't bubbling up in time to fill the gap. Emily tried to fill it for him: "You and I both know there's more to life than our busy little plans. You avoided that for so long. I'm happy you want to know more. I just don't want to lose you, is all."

Popey leaned into her slightly, and nearly whispered, "You never will, Em. I will never go away forever, no matter what. Right?" Emily felt her cheeks flush and her eyes grow heavy. "Allright. I understand." Then she picked her head up with a swift determination, kissed Popey on the cheek, and hugged him even harder. "You'll never lose me, either. If you don't come back, I'll find you."

They stayed embraced for a long time, and Lilly started to grow impatient. She finally interrupted, "Popey, we do have some, ah, work to do," and Popey got the message. He said a soft, "Goodbye" as if he had made his mind up, and Emily echoed it back. She let him go backing away, and then swiftly turned to run. Through the back of her head, Popey could feel her crying, and he felt a tear run down his own cheek.

Lilly looked at him like she never had before. It was almost as if he were a stranger, but the way her eyes longed for more it was obvious she cared deeply for him. "Come on, Popey, let's go home and relax. It's been another long day." After bidding Misha goodbye, off they went to Lilly's house.

The rest of the day Popey sat still in the comfortable chair, thinking about what he was going to do. He honestly didn't know for sure. Lilly knew better than to ask him, and she busied herself cleaning and arranging. For supper, she made a grasshopper mouse roast that was the best Popey had ever eaten. They spoke nothing but idle chatter the whole time. After dinner they sat by the fire, and Lilly spoke first:

"So what are you thinking, Popey?"
"I dunno. I guess nothing, nothing at all."
"Aren't you worried?"
"About what?"
"Things, you know, what you're going to... do?"
"I really don't care anymore. As The Book says, 'Once a Hopneg has no fear, he has nothing left in his mind.'"
"Does The Book really say that?"
"No, I made it up," Popey smiled.
"Maybe it's time we all went to bed. It was a long day."
"I think you may be right. I am very tired, in a way."
"Goodnight, Popey. I'd like to talk in the morning."
"Goodnight, Lilly, I'm sure we will."

And with that Popey crawled into bed, and fell asleep hard and fast. The same dream burst back into his head again, where he is standing facing what he now knew was the dawn. Someone called his name, but he didn't turn around. He didn't even want to. He kept looking straight ahead at the improbable colors that rose each day, and watched the cordgrass wave at them. The wind gently brushed his cheek. As the light increased, a wood duck called and rose in flight. The light made him unafraid. And Popey took a step forward, a step not carefully placed at all.

In the morning, Popey woke up before the dawn. He went outside, and felt the warmth rise on his skin. Everything was laid out before him, just like in his dream. And he knew what he was going to do.

CHAPTER 6:
CONSIDER BEGINNINGS

By the time Popey came back from seeing his dream rise in front of him, the warm smell of breakfast greeted him at Lilly's door. He opened it carefully, not sure what to tell his sister. But his nose moved ahead of him anyway. He slipped past the door, letting the grass seed porridge lead the way. Sitting at the table with a forced smile, he decided that breakfast had to come first, and then news. Some things need a full belly, after all.

Lilly asked Popey how he slept, and he told her that he felt really great and refreshed. Her smile showed how worried she was that he was in some kind of shock; rest was the only cure for that. They sat down and ate without talking, a silence that slowly got louder and louder between them.

Once he was done, Popey started cleaning up. "Thanks for a great breakfast, as usual, Sis."
"Oh, you know how I love to do that for you, Popey. It's going to be a busy day, and we need our bellies full!"
"Yes, Lilly, about that, I have something I want to tell you."
Lilly shrank back as if danger was approaching. "Yes, Popey?"
"Lilly, I have decided I need to go. Go off on my own for a while, see things. I hope you understand."
"No, Popey, I don't," Lilly dropped her bowl in frustration, "Not at all. There's no reason to feel embarrassed by all the things that have happened, you can rebuild! We're all about to lose our houses, you know!"
"It's not about that, Lilly"
"And you don't need to be embarrassed by that... plan of yours. No harm was done to anyone!"
"It's not that, either. I just think it's time that someone... me, really... I want to know more about what's going on, what it's all about."
"That's what the elders are for! You can learn from Misha!"

"Misha admitted that she's... well... limited. That was really what convinced me. Don't you see, Lilly, that there's things going on that none of us really know anything about! We have to stop running all the time!"

"You're running, aren't you?" Lilly shot back. With that, Popey felt a large, friendly smile drift across his face. He was solid in his purpose, but very happy for it. Happy down to his warm, full belly.

"I'm not going to run, I'm going to walk."

Lilly let this comment fly over her and disappear. It was obvious that she wasn't going to understand this no matter what. Her eyes filled with tears as she sputtered out, "This is so hard, so terribly hard, Popey."

Popey put his arm around his sister and hugged her gently. "Everything is hard, Lilly. Taking that first step will be hard. But after many more, it will be easy."
"Where will you go?"
"I think I will walk towards where the Giants live, rather than away. You can all resettle in the fields up the river, but I'd like to see what's downriver."
Lilly pushed herself away from Popey's arm.
"Why, Popey, why? That's dangerous!"
"It may be. But it's dangerous everywhere. Danger is just what you aren't used to."

Lilly still had no idea what was happening around her, but she could tell that her brother had his mind made up. He was as hardheaded as she, after all. She turned around and opened up her cabinets frantically, trying to find something.

"Popey, send word back, will you? There are a lot of Travelers who can send word back to us and let us know how you are."
"I will, Sis. And I will come back one day and find you."
Lilly finally seemed to find what she was looking for, and shook out a large dark green blob with a thwack! that cut the heavy air.
"Take this, if you must go. It's my old heavy cloak. The color will hide you from a lot of danger when you need it."
"Thank you, Lilly, thank you very much. I suppose this is all I have now, other than these pajamas."

They stood there a moment, looking for words. Popey was just glad that with this present Lilly seemed to be accepting the situation. He didn't want to just sneak off on her, not without saying a proper goodbye. When Lilly was done fussing with the cloak she gave it to Popey who put it on with a fancy swirl over his head. It was large and warm and fit him well.

"Shame I don't need these great pockets, since I don't have anything!" Popey laughed as he stuck them out with his playful hands. Lilly gasped a quick, "Oh!" and ran to her pantry. She pulled out two large bags of roasted seeds that were one of Popey's favorite snacks. "Take these, they'll fill up those pockets."

"Thanks, Lilly, this is great." As Popey kept fumbling with the cloak, he pulled it all around himself to see how really big it was. It covered him totally. It was just what the Traveler needed.

They stood there a moment, not knowing what to say before goodbye. Lilly finally cut the silence by asking, "Are you going to say goodbye to Misha... or Emily?" Popey thought a moment, and told her, "I did, already. Thanks. I guess it's time to go."

Lilly finally gave in to her feelings and hugged her brother tightly. She sobbed gently, sure that she'd never see him again. They stood there a long time, in the space between her kitchen and dining room, feeling as though the world might well be ending. But Popey only became more excited as he thought about what was ahead. He kissed his gently on the forehead, and said, "Goodbye Lilly. Thanks for everything, I really mean it. It's just time for me to be alone for a while."

And with that, he pried Lilly off of himself and made for the door. He paused just a moment to say one last "Goodbye" before leaving, but Lilly was crying too hard to say anything. Popey slipped out through the door and was gone.

The first footstep was not as hard as he thought, and each one became easier. One by one they came, and a warm glow rose through his small frame. Once out of the grove, he followed the small path that he was told led to the river.

At a clearing in the cordgrass, he felt the sun sparkle on his right cheek. He paused a moment to look back, and saw only the tall stand of oaks that he knew as home. A bobbing and cheering crowd of grasses waved him on, and he turned again to the path. Each step was easier. Each heartbeat fell with his feet in perfect time. The gentle smile that drew across his face was the only part of him not tight with the rhythm of his feet.

The air was cool and gently fluttering. The world had just started to come alive, with the damp smell of dawn lingering underneath. A few finches chirped excitedly, finding their breakfast. But everything else was still and gentle. Popey had nothing to concentrate on other than his footsteps, one after the other, in a constant beat.

When he reached the end of the field after two handspans of sun, the cottonwoods greeted him like an old friend. This was strange, since he had never been this far before. But the shade and cover they offered was cool and inviting. He paused only a moment, to find the path, and then slipped in to the shade.

After marching along without thinking for a while, he came to place where the path he was on crossed another. He had not thought this would happen. In his dream, the way seemed obvious. But here on these paths it was not. All Popey could think of was to continue the way he knew, with the dawn to his right, until he found the river he'd heard so much about. After that, he could turn into the dawn and follow the river down.

Perhaps it was obvious, but he thought about the other path for a while. After all, what was it? 'Whatever,' he decided, and made off for the river. He was focused on his goal now, nothing could stop him.

The path became a bit narrower, and obviously less traveled. Worse, there was mud all over that stuck to Popey's feet. Eventually, each step became heavier and heavier until it seemed like this nasty path was not going to get him anywhere good in the near future. After slogging and squishing away with determination for a long time, Popey found himself nearly exhausted. His feet were filthy and heavy, caked with mud. As he stood there a moment looking at the mess, wildly trying to snatch his breath, a blue hopelessness rose in him.

Popey could hear nothing but the sound of his own breath, and how his heartbeat echoed in his ears. And he stood there a moment, sinking slightly into the muck, he tried to check out the scene. He didn't notice until he stopped that an awful, rotting smell had closed around him. There wasn't anything alive or moving – only cottonwoods and ferns. But just as desperation was getting to him, his breath quieted and his heartbeat fell slightly. And that's when he heard it.

Off in front of him, there was a great roar, a slurp, an echo of many different sounds boiling and rolling together. Could that be it? Could he have finally found the river?

With a squishy yank on his left foot he pulled it out of the muck, and then came the right. Each one popped slightly from all the mud on it. But once they were free, Popey found himself running as hard as he could, pushing mud behind in his growing wake. His heart rose again, but this time the feeling was not panic but joy. The river! It is here! I have found it! Through the clearing and up the rise and... there...

A huge lake rose in front of him, much bigger than he expected. It was only after he stopped and caught his breath that he could see logs and other things moving slowly on to his right. That was the way down the river, as he was told. But the river itself was such a massive, rolling brown thing! It seemed to be alive in its own way, not moving unless you stopped to see its breath and feel its heartbeat. It was so large that Popey could not clearly make out the other side. And its roar was so deafening that as he tried to find his own breath, Popey couldn't hear himself. This was much larger than he had been told, much more of everything.

He stood there a long time, trying to understand this thing. It was at the same time frightening and calming. Popey remembered being on top of the hood of the Demon, and how the lightening was running through his veins in the excitement of the moment. This was just as terrifying, yet somehow different. Large as it was, it belonged here, it shaped the whole valley in which he had been born.

As it slurped and sucked on the edges, small fish darted in and out of Popey's view. A damp breeze was pulled along with the water, and caught him on the cheek. There was so much alive here, even things that weren't really alive.

It puzzled Popey how he never came here before, how he'd somehow missed this large thing. And he realized he was told to fear this river and how dangerous it was. He snorted at the thought, and smiled out at the river moving on yet never really moving in front of him. Dangerous? It may be, but it also was the most amazing thing he had ever seen.

After standing on the bank a long time, drinking all of this in, Popey realized that the path ended where he stood. The land he was on was swallowed up by the river just a short distance downstream. There was nowhere to go except into this great thing, and he had no idea how to do that. It was either that, or go back.

He fished into his pockets and grabbed a seed. This was as good of a time for lunch as any. He sat down, and nibbled and chewed until his belly was stuffed. This gave him time to sink in a bit and feel the river until he let his mind flow along with it. The gurgles and spits became friendlier and friendlier to him; besides, he was thirsty. He wandered up to the water, and squatted down to drink. He cupped a handful of the brown water, and found that it was clear up close. As he drank it, he realized it tasted a bit foul and earthy, like a well going bad. But it was what he needed.

He sat a while longer on the sandy shore right by the river, and thought about what he would have to do. Since he could not see any way across, he would have to go back. Now that he found this gentle and terrible river, he wanted to move down it. But he couldn't. The world was so much bigger, so much more divided up than he hoped. It hurt him, but he would have to find that crossing again.

A long time passed before he stretched himself to his feet. A shaft of sun poked through the trees from the top of the sky, slightly pointing the way back. He would just follow the sun for a while and see where it took him. That meant back through the cottonwoods, back through the mud.

He trudged his way through, much more bitter about it the second time. Where do these paths go? Am I lost already, so close to home? By the time he got to the crossing, he was exhausted, more from worry and confusion than just the mud. He sat there a while, cleaning his feet and thinking.

Just then, a dark figure showed up on of the path that came out of the woods. It was another Hopneg, he thought, by the way it walked and the size. Yes, it was, some guy in black – Popey made out his long cloak and soon his dark hair and bulging backpack. Was this a Traveler? It certainly looked like the ones he'd seen before. He stood a moment to get a better look.

"Hello!" Popey called out. He wanted to make sure he was friendly. "Why hello, kid, what's up?" The man was close enough to flash some teeth in a wide smile that showed he had a cool, easy way.

"Not much, I guess" Popey lied.
"Catch anything good?"
"What?"
"Didja catch anything decent while you were fishing?"
"Fishing? No, I just went to... to look at the river. I'd never seen it before."
'Oh, well that's basically a fishing path, though it's hard to catch anything in the spring it's so fast. And there's all that mud." He pointed to Popey's feet.
"Yeah, this isn't very much fun." Popey was getting impatient.
"So you live here, kid?"
" I did. I decided to go out traveling for a while."
"Why is that?"
"They're all moving on because they're afraid of the Giants. I just don't want to join them. I want to learn more about the Giants and... well, other magic. You know about these things?"
The man laughed a hearty laugh. Popey could see he was not old, but not a kid anymore, and had a nice beard that made his open mouthed laugh seem bigger. "I know about a lot of things. My

name is Shajee, by the way." He had reached where Popey was standing and thrust out his arm to shake hands.

"Uh, I'm Popey. Sorry, I didn't introduce myself." He winced a bit from Shajee's grip.
"First rule of being a Traveler, kid, is don't apologize for anything. Unless you have to, of course." That gleaming grin never stopped.
"Thanks. Can you tell me the way downriver?"
"Sure, I'm going there. Why do you want to go there?"
"This path, this cross path, is the way?"
"It is. Why you want it?"
"Well, I want to learn about the Giants and all, find out about..."
"You want to learn about stuff. Well, everyone else here is running."
" I don't want to run. It's so... stupid, really. Someone needs to know about these things and maybe we won't have to run."

Shajee paused for a moment, sizing up this new friend. He liked Popey, even if he was a little serious. That would change, he figured, and this kid would make a fine partner. Even if he didn't know better than to stay out of the mud.

"Kid, if we're going to go the same direction I'd be happy to have the company. Besides, you don't sound like you're any competition for the jewels and stuff I'll collect."
"Jewels? Is that why you're going that way?"
"No other reason, since there's hardly any other Hopnegs. They all bailed out long ago. But the stuff you can find, man! Whew!"
"So this is it, this is like the last town before... the Giants and all?"
"Just about. And your people are bailing, too. This time of year it's good to trade jewels, as people like their stuff more portable. Lots of movement. Lots of them fleeing."

Popey thought for a moment. "So this happens to us everywhere?"
"Oh, sure kid. We all move around a lot... have to. Just some of us take to the nature of things better than others and keep only what we can carry." Shajee patted his pack at the last comment almost lovingly, like it was a symbol of who he was. But Popey couldn't think of what to say, and just wanted to get going. "So this is the

path that follows the river?" Shajee smiled again at how focused his new friend was.

"Yes, it is. It stays back from the river most of the way, though."
"Will we see the river again?"
"Sure will, in time. So you want to come with?"

Popey tried his best to match the glittering grin. "Yes, I'd like that very much."

Chapter 7:
Mindful of Little Things

One foot in front of the other. That was the only sound for the longest time as they marched down the path. At first, Popey felt his heart beat in time to his steps and his breath float above the rhythm. But in time, even that was forgotten. His first step down the path was long behind him. He moved on without even thinking.

The trees and brush were thick on this path. Since the sun did not come through, Popey had no way of knowing how much time was passing. The huge cottonwoods, so big he could not see the tops, covered and shielded them. The path itself had to run around a smaller forest of saplings that stood everywhere. In time, these would grow to replace the larger ones. But for now, some were not much bigger than the pair of hikers dodging them. Popey smiled at the idea of them being his size and yet so big one day soon. All would change with time.

They both kept on this way for a long time, not saying a word. Eventually, the silence stood between them like a third companion. Popey's deep sense of wonder at the forest gave way to realizing that Shajee was over there, not saying anything either. It was awkward and deep.

But the damp, cool air was great for hiking, and they put a lot of cottonwoods behind them in no time. It was just this forest, for the longest distance, and nothing else at all. They were the only ones out there, making time down the path. Sometimes a vole might rustle to the side, or a small bird might call high above. Most of the time, though, it was just the two of them and the silence between them, Popey usually a half step back. It was exciting in still another different way – a quiet and thoughtful excitement.

The thick air was suddenly cut by Shajee announcing, "Let's take a break here on this log". Nothing more was said until they sat down, and Popey fished in his pockets for a seed. He realized that he was more thirsty than hungry, but had no water with him. "You... have any water I could... borrow?" he asked tentatively.

"Sure, have some of mine. Shajee gave him the canteen he just fished out of his pack.

"Thanks, I really appreciate it. I guess I forgot to ask for a canteen."

"Ask who?"

"My sister. She gave me the coat."

"Oh. Well, you can have that one, you'll need it."

"Really? You don't need it?"

"Naw, I have spares, kid. Gotta be prepared."

"Wow, thanks."

The silence closed in around them suddenly as Popey realized he must look like an idiot. How could you go traveling with nothing? After a time, he felt he had to say something to redeem himself.

"Would you like one of my seeds? They're real fresh."

"Thanks, that's nice of you, kid. Nice pockets you have, real useful."

Popey blushed when he realized that Shajee sensed his embarrassment and was trying to be nice to him to cover it. He wondered what else this man knew about him, and what he was thinking about during their hike.

"Thanks, I guess I could have been better prepared than just this."

"No sweat, kid. But you could use a pack, maybe, somewhere down the path."

"Yeah, that'd be nice Shajee. I didn't... well, I didn't plan for this. I thought it would be kind of easy and all."

"Everything is hard if you make it hard, kid. Everything is easy if you just realize that and keep it straight in your mind." He tapped his temple with a pointed finger and laughed carelessly at that last thought.

"I'll remember that, thanks."

"So this is all you have, kid? What happened to you?"

"Um, a Demon destroyed everything I had. I barely escaped."

"So that's why you're out walking, kid. Well, I knew you weren't a punk."

"How did you know that?"

"You think about stuff. And your hands show you aren't afraid of work."

"You can tell all that?"

"Sure, kid. You can tell a lot by keeping your eyes open. That's how it is as a Traveler, you have to know what's up and go along with it. All it takes really is looking."

Popey realized that back during that period of heavy silence Shajee was figuring him out. All of the time that Popey was watching the trees, Shajee had him pegged perfectly. And he didn't have to say a word, or at least anymore than he had said when they first met.

"Well, thanks for saying I'm not a punk, Shajee. I do appreciate that."

"I'll bet you got a load from the people in town when you lost all your stuff."

"I sure did."

"Is that really why you left, kid?"

"Well, sort of… I mean, it just didn't seem like very important magic, what with the Demon taking it so easily and all."

"Let me tell you something. Magic isn't here in this pack of mine, it's here." He pointed to Popey's temple this time. When Popey looked confused, Shajee dropped his head back and laughed up at the far tops of the trees. It was a big, echoing laugh that almost sounded like a challenge to the big cottonwoods.

"You know, kid, I mean it when I say people make things hard for themselves. You've seen that. All this 'magic' they say they have, what was it good for?"

"That's exactly what I thought!" Popey shot back with his hands waving

"You figured it out, kid, and that's great. But most of them won't. You had to lose everything to figure it out, right?"

"Yeah, well… pretty much. I mean, I thought about this stuff a lot before, but I just didn't say anything. Except to Em."

"Your girl?"

Popey looked to the ground for a good answer to that.

"Ah, well… sort of. I dunno. She listened a lot, we talked about dreams and stuff. That was what we thought was the real magic, I guess."

"Well, kid, you were a lot closer to being right than the others."

Popey lifted his head slowly and looked at Shajee. That wide grin never quit. He felt like he had to say something, but the right word wasn't there.

"Thanks. I appreciate it," was all that came out.

"Don't worry, kid, you've got the right idea. You're just going with the flow, and you'll learn a lot. Just going back to the places we don't go to anymore will teach you a lot of what you want to know."

"You think so?"

"I'm sure of it. You got the right idea."

"You think we can fight the Giants, then?"

"Well, kid, maybe you don't really have the right idea yet. But I think it's deep inside of you all the same."

"What does that mean?"

"I think you'll see. There's something up ahead that might get you going. Let's go, it's getting late."

Popey wanted to talk some more, and getting back on the trail seemed to mean that they couldn't talk. That was only because the last time they were walking they said nothing, he realized. Getting up didn't really mean the conversation had to end. Popey stuffed his new canteen into a pocket and followed behind the dark cloak of Shajee, struggling to keep up for a moment.

When he was alongside Shajee, and fell into a rhythm, Popey hesitated to talk. It seemed strange. But he finally pushed aside the silence that had joined them before and just started babbling.

"What did you mean there's something ahead?"

"Well, lots of things, kid, but one I'd like to make before nightfall."

"It will change my mind about something."

"Yeah, about Giants. And the world, who knows?"

"You mean I'll like them or something?"

"No, just not fear them so much. Fear is one of those things that makes everything harder than it should be."

Popey found a sudden twinge in his guts. He had more in common with Shajee than he thought. There was also a lot more to the life of the Travelers than he thought, too. They talked on in little bits for a while, mostly because Popey wanted to break the silence for good. But it was nothing but small talk, how to recognize trails and related Traveler wisdom that fell between them. But Popey was warmed by all of it, by the world being so much bigger than he ever imagined. Being only three and a quarter inches tall seemed like it was very important, and then not so important at the same time.

After they had plodded along for what seemed like forever, Popey realized that he knew nothing about Shajee and where he came from. He was about to ask him, when a sudden blast of warmth fell on his back. The sun! They were out of the forest and into a clearing. That was when Shajee shouted, "There it is!"

Ahead of them were nothing but rocks, grass, and a huge straight mountain. The mountain was arranged like a whole bunch of canteens stuck together. It was thick and whitish-gray, and perfectly smooth up the sides. Popey had never seen a mountain before, but had heard of them in stories.

"We'll make a camp here by the clearing, and then attack at night." Shajee said as he slid his pack off and onto a log.
"Attack? The mountain?" Popey was excited about doing something to get back at the Giants, but this did seem a bit crazy.
"No, kid, I'll show you. But first, I think we need some shelter. I have a feeling it may rain tonight."

With that, Shajee pulled a small saw out of his pack and went to work on one of the saplings nearby. After it was felled, he called to Popey to give him some help with it. "I'll show you how to make camp. I'm sure you can be a lot of help." And with that Shajee carefully showed Popey just where to place the saplings to make a strong frame. They then made the roof, using broad cottonwood leaves for the thatching and ripped other varieties to make string from the veins.

When it was finished, they had an open shelter with a broad sloping roof that was waterproof. It would hold both of them easily, no matter what happened that night, and protect them. There was even a place for a partially sheltered fire ring, which Popey collected stones to finish.

"There we have it! You now know how to make a real Traveler shelter, kid."

"I sure could use a saw like that one before I make one on my own, though."

"We'll deal with that later. First, aren't you hungry?"

The thought had crossed Popey's mind several times while building the shelter. But now he was so tired from worry and walking and wonder and work that he didn't realize he was hungry until Shajee said something.

"Yeah, I could use something."

"Well, it's probably dark enough, kid. I think we can go get it. Follow me!"

"Where are we going? Are we going to attack now?"

"Not attack, that's just a way of saying things. It's more like we're going to clean things up a bit."

Popey followed, but he didn't like the sound of this. He wasn't used to all the walking he'd done, but was ashamed to admit he was too tired for more work. Attacking might be one thing, that'd be glorious, but cleaning? Whatever the deal, Shajee hadn't been wrong yet. Popey followed more out of curiosity than anything else.

They skirted the edge of the clearing carefully, looking out over the rocks and grass to the mountain far away. It was slightly to the south of the camp, and as the pair got around the clearing the sun was setting. The failing orange glow lit up one side of the mountain, but left the other in darkness. When Popey glanced over to see that they were still safe, the mountain stood there half lit, half dark. It was all one mountain, though, much like the last time Popey saw this, when the light and dark were both falling on him.

"Shajee, is that mountain something the Giants made?"

"Why, yes it is, kid. It's not really a mountain, but their storage bin."

"They have food in there for the winter?"

"They have it in there all the time, I dunno why. But we don't have to go there, there's a better place. Through here."

They came to a huge wall of wire that was tangled up like it was twisted together. The holes between it were easy to get through, but the wall itself was huge and obviously protected something valuable. Popey noticed a large sign to one side, like the Giants always use for their magic. He was going to ask about it, but keeping up with Shajee was so difficult he forgot.

After they cleared the wall, they marched on for quite a while. Then, the trees parted and a familiar whooshing sound hit Popey's ears. "There's the river you asked about. And just ahead is what I was after."

There was a series of large buildings and tubes all over the place, and in the river sat some enormous metal boats. The size of it all made Popey stop for a moment, but then he had to race to catch up to Shajee. He had made it down on the riverbank, which was very steep now. "Here it is, kid! All you can eat. Just fill those pockets of yours and we'll have a feast tonight!"

There, on the ground, was scattered all over what looked like seeds. They were a strange orange color, much like the setting sun that was disappearing fast. Shajee seemed sure they were good to eat, so Popey did what he was told. After a while of scampering around, they had all they could carry.

"Let's get back to camp, kid, it's getting dark." And it was, fast.

On the way out through the wall, Popey remembered to ask about the sign. "Can you... do you know what this says, what magic it has?"
"Sure, kid. It says 'Grain Terminal'" That's what we have here is grain they didn't want for some reason. Maybe they just overlooked it."
"You can read, Shajee?"
"Sure can, kid. Well, sort of anyways. Travelers can all read some."
"Have you ever read The Book?"
"Well... yeah, a little. It says some good things, for sure. Why do you ask?"
"Well, in my town, only a few people could read it, or read anything."

"Yeah, that's town people for you."

"What do you mean?"

"I mean that you let other people be in charge too much, let them run everything. Even if they don't do any work."

"That's what Rod said."

"Well Rod was right, kid. I'll bet he was a pretty good guy, then."

Popey didn't respond to that. They were at camp, and he knew there was more to this than gathering seeds. Shajee slung off his now bulging sack and lifted out a metal pot and a rod. "You got the grass and twigs to get this going here?" Popey pulled off the ground all the fuel for a decent fire and stacked it just right in the ring. Shajee struck his staff against a rock and the sparks soon caught the grass on fire, then the wood. When it had started to really glow, he got excited and fumbled for his supplies.

"Oh, this will be good, kid. You'll like this. Grain porridge, really good stuff." He filled the pot with a whole canteen of water and started shoveling grain into it, cracking each one open with his hands as he went. "These things are a bit tough, kid, you want to help me here? Just like this. Good."

And when they were done they stirred the coals and set the pot on the rocks to suspend it over the fire. "It's gotta boil first, kid, then we have a good meal." Popey was now so hungry he didn't want to wait, but in no time the pot was boiling.

When it had bubbled a short time, Shajee lifted it off and poured the now thick mass into two metal cups he fished out of his pack. "Hope you like it, kid!" he said as he lifted his cup. Popey drank quickly out of hunger, and it was very good. It may have been the best meal he'd ever had. The long day of walking had him totally wiped out. The porridge warmed him in a way that made him sleepy and satisfied. Any doubts he had left about what he was doing drained down into his full guts.

"Shajee, that was great, but I'm really tired. I need to sleep."

"Long day traveling, eh kid? I'm tired too. The rest of this is gonna be great cold for breakfast."

"I sleep over here?"

"Wherever you want, kid. You have a good night. If it rains we'll deal with that later, but I think we have a good house here." He grabbed the cross support and shook it slightly. Not much moved. "Goodnight, Shajee. And thanks, thanks a lot."
"Goodnight, kid"

And with that, Popey lay down and pulled his sister's cloak tight around him. He arranged some of the grass beside him into a pillow, and fell asleep on it immediately.

CHAPTER 8:
NOT DOING

When Popey woke up, the sun was already peering over the distant trees that ran along the river. He was glad to have the rest, but embarrassed to find Shajee already awake and stirring up the cold porridge. The morning was cold and heavy in his nose, but dry except for the dew.

"Morning. Guess it didn't rain after all, kid."
"Good morning, Shajee." Popey stretched his sore body. "No, it seems dry."
"Better prepared than not. Building a house like this is easy, but getting wet is hard. You want breakfast cold, or you want to warm it up?"
"Cold sounds good. I'd like to try it, anyways."
"Sure thing, kid. Here you go."

Popey twisted up to a sitting position, and snatched the cup quickly. He was very hungry. Slurping down the porridge was almost as warming as it had been the night before. He ate it quick and noisily, as if he might never have another meal again. Shajee looked in amusement, and laughed heavily.

"I was surprised at how well you kept up with me, kid, but I can see now it was a bit hard on you for a first day."
Popey lowered his cup for just a moment, and Shajee grabbed it to refill it with what was left.
"What do you mean?"
"Well, kid, you never lagged behind even a fast pace, but the way you slept and the way you are eating... well, it took a toll."
Popey blushed at being measured so carefully.
"Yeah, well, I can keep up, I just need to recharge a bit."
"You're the kind that goes on raw determination, aren't you?"
"I guess... yeah, if I have to."
"That's good, but you have watch yourself."

Popey was tired of talking about himself, and besides that had a fresh cup of porridge in his hand. This one slurped down as quickly as the last and left no time for words. Shajee paused a moment, and then went about the business of cleaning up his pot and packing it away.

"From here out it gets a little dicey at times, so it's good you rested up. We'll have to keep our eyes open."
"What do you mean, dicey?"
"Well, kid, I mean there's a lot of stuff that could make a problem."
"Like?"
"Places we could be seen, things that get dangerous. Like that."
"Right, well… let me know, and I'll watch."
"Will do, kid."

Popey stood up, and wondered what he should be doing to break camp. Shajee had so many things to clean and put in his pack, and all Popey had were his pockets. They still had some seeds in them, the canteen he was given, and a lot of nothing. He was ready to go just by getting up.

"Shajee, can I do something to help?"
"You can wreck the house, kid. Don't want Giants seeing it."
"Seems a shame to waste all that work, though" Popey grabbed the main support and pulled it out of its lashing.
"Eh, you'd have felt different if we got wet. It's allright."

Soon, they were ready to go. Shajee swung his pack over his shoulders, and the weight of it landed on his back with a thud. The force of it hitting knocked the huge grin back on his face, as if in surprise. "Gotta lot of stuff in here, you know it," he told Popey, "Let's go!" And they started walking again over to where the grain and the River were.

The sun had just come up in the sky, and the whole setting looked much different in the light. It was dirtier and dimmer, with the feeling of a place that no one cared about much. The Mountain, still imposing, seemed much more cold and indifferent. Popey made a point of turning away, as he felt he was supposed to, and not looking at it as they made their way past.

Soon, they were beyond the wall and back at the place where the grain was scattered on the ground. Some grasshopper mice had left their tracks around, showing that this was a favorite spot of theirs as well. Popey was studying them as he walked when Shajee announced the plan.

"We need to fill the canteens, and fill your pockets with grain again. There won't be a feast like this for a while."

Shajee led Popey down to a spot where the River was reachable. The cool breeze that followed it caught the pair just as they passed the trees. The River was still alive in so many ways, and the roaring sucking sound was the only thing that cut through the wind. They reached a small beach area, and Shajee started filling his canteens. Popey followed and did the same.

"Not the best water, kid, but it'll keep us going."
"I tasted it before, it does taste like a bad well."
"There's better to be had later. Still might as well fill up, since we can always dump it."
"Shajee, this path that follows the River, why does it stay so far away from the River itself?"
"Take a look, kid. See how nasty this thing can get?"

Popey looked out at the rolling brown mass, and realized that anything that got too close could be in trouble. He also remembered the mud he was stuck in before.

"I guess, but it seems so far away. Except here."
"There are places we can reach it, and we can make use of them."
"It is dangerous then, isn't it?"
"Sure is, kid. Wait until we cross it."

And with that, Shajee turned and flashed his big grin again. He wanted to see what Popey thought of this, but Popey was just blank. Crossing this thing seemed impossible. Then again, Shajee knew what he was doing and had brought them this far.

It was only after this shock that Popey realized that Shajee had filled no less than five canteens, some of which were very large and hidden in his pack. He had a lot of things with him, and was prepared for everything. Popey's blank look rolled into a smile that nearly matched Shajee's big grin at the thought that maybe things really were that simple, after all.

Once they were fully watered and had washed down their breakfast, they both made their way up to where the grain was scattered. Shajee told Popey to work fast, since the Giants would be there soon at the start of the day. They filled everything they had with grain, and Popey's pockets bulged in an awkward way. With that, they made their way over to the edge of the forest, found a path, and disappeared into the cottonwoods once again.

It was good to be walking again, and the morning air still lingered in the dark forest. With the happy chirps of a few birds and their own feet hitting the path the only sounds, they moved on. The second day was easier, by far.

The silence between them suddenly started to bother Popey again. This day he decided to not let it be a problem again, so he spoke up.

"Shajee, you said that the place by the mountain would change my feelings about Giants. Why was that?"
"Well, kid, you wanted to defeat them, right?"
"And I still do, for all they've done to us!" Popey was angry.
"Did you see how big things were in their world?"
"Yes, they are Giants."
"No, it's more than that, kid. See how much bigger than them it all is?"

Popey fumbled for a while before he could answer. He had no idea where this was going. "Yeah, I see. But what about it?"
"Kid, they have to feel pretty small, too. Alongside that Mountain, that is. But they learned to deal with it."
"You said they made it, that it was their grain bin!"
"Just because they made it doesn't mean it doesn't become their master, too. Kid, there are a lot of ways you can get yourself into trouble."
"What do you mean?"
"I mean that things that big they don't run anymore, they don't control. They deal with it. Just like we did picking up what they dropped."

Popey saw what Shajee meant, and wanted to argue with him. He just couldn't find the words to do it properly.

"I guess... I see what you mean, but... isn't that how they wind up hurting us, too?"
"Sure is, kid. I don't think anyone has control over anything anymore, as if they ever did."
"And don't you want to do something about it?!" Popey was shouting now.
"I see how to live off of it, and I get by. You have to admit, that was some good stuff we ate last night."

This did not sit well with Popey, but he wasn't sure why. Shajee had learned to live with all of these things, Giant made and not. In some ways, he was like Rouger with all his stuff in the pack and how he didn't care about the rest of the world. But Shajee was so much kinder and friendlier all the same. He had his life somehow figured out, and in control, but he was still a decent person.

Thinking about this reminded Popey of Lilly. He missed his sister terribly, and wondered what she was doing right now. Probably, she would be directing the work of moving the seed gathering bins and equipment to some other place. What other place would they go to? Popey realized that he didn't stay around long enough to find out what the plan was. When he got back, they would be gone. Somewhere, just gone.

"You got silent all of a sudden, kid. The porridge so good I won an argument?"
"What? Oh, no... I mean, yes it was good, I was just thinking."
Shajee flashed his teeth again, "I'm just kidding. I don't get into arguments enough to win 'em anyways."
"I do see what you mean, Shajee, but I really don't like it somehow."
"I can tell, you're a thinker. A lot of townies are. That's why that life isn't for me, kid."

Popey liked being called 'a thinker'. All his life he'd been known as just a strong back and pair of arms. It never occurred to him to even try to think, except when he and Em were talking about things.

"Shajee, I just want to figure things out. You know a lot, and really help me with that. I don't know that I'm going to get what I want with the stronger magic and stuff. But I have to try."

"Because you want to take on the Giants, still?"

"Well... yeah, or at least learn how to deal with them without running."

"Wait until you see what's ahead, kid."

"Another Mountain?"

"Of sorts, yeah."

With that, they kept walking on all day long without talking much more about difficult topics. There was plenty of time for Traveler stories and jokes, but mostly they didn't say much along the path after that. Popey wanted to ask what was ahead, but he figured that Shajee would just smile at him again no matter what. It was better to get some of the funny stories down, he could tell them later.

Just as the forest started to thin a bit, Popey noticed that there was no sun poking through the trees. The sky was gray above the canopy. Shajee noticed it, too, and suddenly barked out a command, "Let's pick up the pace, we're almost there!"

They broke into a rough run, a staggering jog made clumsy from a long day's walk. A few drops of rain fell through the trees, spurring them on. Popey felt the determination rise in him, even though he didn't know where he was going. He trusted Shajee so much now, he had fallen back to doing what he was told. When he realized this, he felt stupid and angry about it. But he also knew it had to be done.

Just as the run had left him nearly exhausted, the cottonwoods broke into a clearing. Shajee shouted again, "We're here! We made it!" But Popey had no idea what this place was.

For what seemed like forever, the land in front of them was an open field of all kinds of strange things. There was no end to it all, just more piles of colors and textures. What was this place?

"Welcome to the dump, kid. This is where the Giants put their trash. There's a lot of great stuff, but we have to find shelter, and fast."

Popey stopped to catch his breath while Shajee made a quick survey of the site. As Popey stared blankly, in front of him were more strange and twisted things. The stench of it grabbed his nose and turned it away for a moment, daring him to look back. When he did, he noticed what he feared the most.

"Demons! Over there, at the end, a whole bunch of them!"
"Relax, kid, they'll go away with the rain. Over here it doesn't smell so bad, let's go!"

They moved quickly again, following the edge to their left. Popey could not believe that all of this was trash and filth. He could not see the far side of it in the thick air. It was as if it were limitless, going on forever. And this was only what they had cast off and were done with. The Demons did retreat away slowly, which gave Popey a chance to replace his fear of them with a fear of the Giants he had not felt before. Everything they did was definitely bigger even than they were. Everything was run by some very powerful kind of... magic? Whatever it was, it was also bigger even than the Giants. Did they really control it?

In a pile of mangled things, some of them fluttering in the wind, Shajee found something he liked. "Let's get this open, kid," he shouted. It was a black box, long but quite narrow, with a strange brown top on it. They were able to knock it over and pry the top off in a hurry. When they looked inside, they found it was metal and strong.

"Kid, can you get up top and I'll hand this lid to you on an angle, right?"

Popey had no idea what Shajee had in mind, but he jumped and hoisted himself up to the top and waited. Shajee gathered several small sticks, and then picked up the lid to hand one end to Popey. "Slide this in place on the edge there, over that lip, good!" and then he propped the bottom open with several of the twigs he held under his arm.

Popey stood for a moment on the top of this black box, and saw it was covered white and gold writing. At the top, there was a strange picture that had two animals on it, one on each side. Popey recognized them from pictures he had seen before. The rain had just started to fall when Shajee called, "Allright, kid, come down now. We have a home!"

The box with the propped open lid was just the right size for them to lie down in, but just barely. The sound of rain hitting the metal became a terrible roar, and neither of them spoke as they caught their breath. They were dry, just barely.

"Got in just in time, kid."
"Shajee, what is this place?"
"The dump, I told you, it's where they put all the stuff they don't want."
"And this box?"
"Who knows? They didn't want it anymore, so it's ours."
"I saw a picture on it, with what I think is a Lion and a Unicorn."
"Oh, so that's whose it was!"
"It belonged to a Lion and a Unicorn?"
"No, kid, those are both made-up creatures. They are the symbol of the Giant's royalty."
"Royalty? The ones who run everything?"
"I guess they must, kid."
"Why is their symbol two made-up creatures?"

Shajee paused a moment and thought. It wasn't like him to think like that. He usually shot back an answer and grinned. This time, though, the grin was slow in coming. By the time the thought was ready to escape his mouth, a flash of teeth set the way for it.

"That's probably what makes them royalty, you know. It's all made up, kid. It's fake. Like being in charge."
"Like our elder back at River Flats. He was only in charge because people believed in him."
"Yup, kid, like believing in fairy-tale animals. You got that right. It sure must beat doing work, though."

There was a long pause after that, while the rain beat down on the metal box. The noise was deafening, and neither of them tried to talk over it. They just sat there, gathering their breath, waiting. The curved edge of the box made a decent pillow to lean back on, and the length was exactly Popey's height.

Eventually, the rain slowed a bit. The incredible noise became tolerable. Shajee suddenly spoke up, saying, "I like you, kid, you make me think." Popey had no idea what to say. He wanted to change the subject. He also realized that they would have a hard time making a proper dinner in this otherwise comfy home. Popey fished in his coat pockets for a while, and pulled something out.

"Want a seed? I have some for dinner. They're roasted."
"Thanks, kid. You are allright."

After eating up most of Popey's supply, they both slumped down into the box and quietly fell asleep to the gentle patter of rain on metal.

Chapter 9:
Turning Back

Popey woke up in a fit of silence. The musical noise that put him to sleep was over, and the gentle quiet begged for more investigation. It was time to get up.

Shajee was stirring as well, and soon sat up. Both of them said nothing at first, allowing the silence to pour over them. After a while, it was Shajee who spoke first.

"Get a good sleep, kid?"
"Yeah, I did. You?"
"Sure did. We'll need it. Today might be hard, especially with that rain."
"Is traveling always this hard?"
"Well, kid, I was thinking how we had it pretty good. With the luck of this, I mean."

With that, Shajee thwacked the side of the tin house they were in, and it rang gently with an echo of the night before. Then they were both silent, as if preferring the challenge of a quiet morning. Popey fished a few seeds out of his pockets for breakfast, being all they had, and they ate quickly without speaking. Shajee then stood as best he could, hunched over and stretched his large frame over the whole span of the tin.

"Let's get on it, kid. I'd like to see how far we can get."
"Sure. At least we don't have to pack!"
"Hey, you're learning! Yeah, we got the earth at our feet with a bit of luck."
"I wouldn't want the earth anywhere else, I would think."
"Snappy comeback!" Shajee grinned broadly again, "You're allright, kid."

As they flipped off the lid, the thin light of the morning again revealed the piles of garbage all around where they were. The shimmer of thin fog made it less terrible to look at, but gave the stench of it all something like an arm that grabbed their noses and held on tight. They knew they needed to wrestle themselves away from it quickly.

"Let's get moving, kid."
"Is this the worst thing we're going to see?"
"Eh, maybe. There's something else bad up ahead."
As Shajee pointed, they both started walking quickly.

"Dangerous?"
"You know kid, for some reason I don't see any of this as dangerous. I shoulda asked before, you scared by this?"

Popey hadn't thought about being scared at any time before this, but now that it was brought up it all had been a bit frightening. He confessed to Shajee carefully, not wanting to seem wimpy.

"I don't think... scared isn't the word. I guess I was enjoying it all too much to even realize... to think about it."
"Here's the main path, kid. Well, it sounds to me like you're a real traveler at heart."
"I dunno about that. I mean, I know what it's like to be safe, and somehow that's why I want to have... to experience it all."

With this, Popey realized just how muddy everything was. He was in danger of becoming stuck again, mostly because he wasn't paying attention to where he was walking on the path. He stared at his feet now so that he could hop on the worn river stones set into the soft mud. Shajee was paying such close attention to his own feet that he said nothing, and Popey wasn't sure that the dark presence was even listening. But Popey kept talking.

"I guess now that I know the safety I thought we had wasn't all that real, I don't care about danger."
"Well, kid, you still have to keep your eyes open."
"But I'm not afraid."
"Well, good. Let's get out of here and you'll see what's up.

When the sun was up three handspans, the path became less muddy and the stench started to melt with the heat. Traveling gradually became easier, but as usual they said very little the whole way. Drops of rain crashed around them from the tall cottonwoods, gradually soaking them and making them both a bit miserable.

Suddenly, as they climbed a hill, a different stench grabbed their noses. Popey, who had been thinking about what he was afraid of with the steady beat of his footsteps, had a sudden whiff of real terror that made him stop suddenly.

"What is it, kid?"
"That... that smell. It's... one of those Demons! It's like it's followed me all the way here!"
"No, these ones live here. Many of them. And it's OK to be afraid of them. But we just have to be careful. Got it?"
"Sure... ah, yeah, I understand. They're up ahead?"
"That they are, kid. Let's see what they are up to today. Come on."

Shajee led the way up to the top of the hill, and once there they surveyed the land in front of them. The scene was not like anything Popey had ever seen before.

It was relentlessly gray and colorless, with only large yellow Demons that crawled around and belched smoke. It was only from how they traveled that Popey could see there was texture to the land, otherwise so very uniform. There was no sign of life other than the Demons, who scooped up large hunks of gray and carried them to the right and a place where a few buildings stood.

"What is this place, Shajee?"
"Not sure, kid. They seem to be taking away all of this stuff here."

With that, he knelt down and picked up a rock that was the size of his hand, one small part of the gray mass in front of them. He showed it to Popey as if it was one of the treasures in his pack, grinning broadly the whole time. Popey spoke first.

"That's a 'keeble'. We used those stones on the farm."
"Thought you said you were from a town, kid."
"Well, yes, but we had a farm on the edge of the town that Lilly, my sister owned. I worked in it all the time, growing seeds."
"And you used these?"

"Well, not just these. I mean, we had the keebles and the drats and all the other sizes. They give you drainage to make fertile land stay in place and work properly."

"So these stones are useful?"

"Well, yes, but... so many? All at once? I don't understand."

"I sure don't either, kid. But you'll see the Giants do everything... well, even bigger than they are."

Popey knew this was right, and was sure it was the real kind of magic that he was looking for all along. But here, on the edge of this gray wasteland, it suddenly didn't look like the kind of magic he wanted to have anything to do with. He stood there, staring at the ugliness of it for what seemed like forever, when Shajee finally spoke.

"Here, kid, take a drink. We'll get more soon. See that large straight thing up ahead, across the river?"

Popey just nodded as he drank, still staring ahead.

"That's where we're going, kid. To get there, off to the left here and we're less likely to be flooded out. Got it?"

"Ah, sure. What are they doing with all this?"

"Like I said, I have no idea."

"All at once, all by itself... this is strange magic here. It makes no sense."

Shajee wanted to pry Popey away, but he realized that a short break after the longer part of the day they'd had wasn't gong to hurt. Besides, this was the kid's first time through the area and he was learning. Those earlier comments about not being scared had Shajee a little worried, like Popey might do something stupid. But now something different hung in the air, a proper respect for the situation that would do well to sink in.

"So, kid, you're a lot quieter than when we first started out."

"Oh, me? Well, I didn't think it would be like this."

"You want to go and take on those Demons? Take on the Giants?"

"What? No... well, I do, actually, but I don't know why."

"What would you do anyways?"

"I don't know. I really don't."

With that last comment, Popey's eyes finally fell off of the scene and onto his worn and swollen feet, still caked with mud. Following his dream suddenly seemed a lot more difficult, and much less rewarding. It used to be enough to have a dream, when he had lost everything. Now, he had to know what it all meant – and it wasn't making any sense at the moment.

Popey looked up again. The sky was deep and blue, and the sun was warming their wet frames. Popey thought about charging the Demons and trying once again to suffocate them, and how foolish it all seemed now. Besides, these were out in the light, and if Hopnegs had learned anything it was how to stay hidden from the Giants. There was no way to charge across the gray without being seen, standing out as the only life in a dead land. Nothing could be more dangerous, nothing seemed more futile. There wasn't even a good reason. But it seemed like something should be done.

When Popey looked back at his feet, he knew that all he could do was keep moving. As his head fell, Shajee took this as a nod.

"Allright, kid. Let's get going. Off here, into the woods again. It'll be safe and dark."
"Sure."
"You OK?"
"Yeah... I'm fine. I just don't understand."

They tramped off together, slipping into the darkness of a canopy of bushes. The path twisted and turned at first, and then became straight and easy. It wasn't wet and muddy, at least. And the darkness suddenly felt warm in a way the sun never could. Shajee felt he had to say something more, but he wasn't used to talking while he walked. But he remembered feeling the same way when he first saw this place, and felt like he had to say more. The words simply failed him, though. Besides, Popey wasn't expecting anything from him.

Still, the third traveler of unspoken thoughts and awkward silences appeared between them again. In a moment, they were both trying to find words to beat this unfriendly character back, and they both spoke at once:

"It's one of those things, kid." "I think I know what bothered me."
"You go first, kid."
"I think I know what bothered me."
"What?"
"It was how gray it was, how totally dead. It just wasn't right."
"I hate to tell you, but we have more of that up ahead."
"What... what do you mean?"
"Well, a lot of gray at least. Not as dead as that place, it creeps me out, too, kid."
"But just as gray and ugly? Up ahead?"
"Yeah, but with a lot of Giants running around."
"Is that the danger you warned me about?"
"Sure is, kid. This is just ugly. Those Demons we can leave alone."

Popey was starting to re-think the feelings he had just this morning. But he also had the feeling that Shajee was deliberately making him do that, and he resented it. He started to wish that Shajee was a bit more descriptive, and told him more.

"How dangerous is this going to get then? I feel like... are you telling me everything I need to know here?"
"I can only tell you so much, kid. You have to see this for yourself to understand it."
"I always heard there were more Giants than you could imagine downriver. Is this really true? Is it going to keep getting worse?"

Shajee sighed, the first time Popey heard that from him. This was getting way deeper than he wanted it to get. He was going to break with his usual routine and give a short speech. He hated doing that. But the kid needed to know to trust himself, and he probably was too tired by now to do it without encouragement. Shajee stopped suddenly, looked at the ground, and looked up at Popey, speaking in a strong voice.

"Kid, listen to me. I can tell you what I think, but I can't tell you what you think. I see things one way, you may see them another. You don't want to think like me, unless'in you want to be a Traveler all the rest of your life. I like your companionship, and I like having you help out. But I'm not a teacher, OK?"

Popey looked right at him, but gradually he realized how his pestering was making Shajee very uncomfortable. Popey's eyes fell once more as a bubble of shame reddened his face. Shajee continued much quieter.

"Listen, kid, if I've learned one thing it's that what's in my head isn't what's out in the world. It's just a… like a description of it, without the pictures. It has what I saw, but not everything. What's in me is me. The world is a lot bigger than that. That's all I'm saying. You gotta see it all."

Popey couldn't stop feeling ashamed, even though he knew that's not what Shajee wanted him to feel. It suddenly dawned on him that his determination of just a few days ago was making it a lot harder on him, and his desire to learn everything at once made it hard to learn anything at all.

"Shajee, I'm sorry. I'm just… I feel like a little kid."
"That's good. A little kid sees everything for the first time."
"What do you mean?"

Shajee looked Popey right in the eyes, and paused a moment. He was debating whether it was time for another speech. Hating the idea of doing that again, he instead spoke quickly and smoothly.
"Soak it all up, kid. You're doing great. Just soak it up like you did when you were little and you'll get it in time."
"OK."

With this, they started walking again. Dodging small saplings and grasses that periodically interrupted the otherwise straight path, they made very good time until they finally heard the familiar roar of the river once again. When they got to the sandy bank, they peered out into the light once again, careful to not be noticed. When all was clear, they dropped down and knelt by the tan colored water to fill all their nearly empty canteens. A small piece of metal stood at the edge of the river, and Shajee snatched it up and put it in his pack.

"Another small treasure!"
"What is it, Shajee?"
"Just Giant stuff, could be useful for digging."

"You mind if I ask you a question?"

"Sure, kid, go ahead."

"I thought you traded jewels and valuables along the path? Where is everyone?"

"Would you get mad if I said you'll see?" Shajee grinned.

"No, I'm OK," Popey grinned right back.

They were silent for a moment as Shajee fixed his pack back up. Then, he pointed behind Popey.

"See that?"

"That huge, straight thing?"

"Yup, that."

"Is that where we are going?"

"Tonight. We don't get to sleep tonight."

"Why?"

"Have to go in the dark. But we'll eat first."

"So we're going over there now?"

"Told you it'd be a long day, didn't I, kid?"

"I'm OK, I can do it."

"We'll sleep when it's over. Take a day off."

With that, they trudged along the sandy shore towards the big, gray thing obviously made by Giants. As they did, a whirring, buzzing noise sang out and a smell like Demons started to fill the air. Popey decided to say nothing, and as they got closer he saw it was indeed all the Giant's work, with their Demons soaring across it at very high speeds. He had no idea what was ahead, but decided it was not time to worry about it. They stopped directly under it.

"Kid, let's get a fire going and crack open some seeds for a good dinner. We'll need it."

With that, Popey set to work and nearly forgot to be worried.

CHAPTER 10:
WATER AND STONE

Together, they cooked up a batch of porridge and ate well. It was all gone in just a few moments. Shajee noted that they still had a lot of grain left, and would be well suited for the days ahead. Since it was not quite dark yet, they had a lot of time before they could attempt to move as planned.

"I'm full up, kid. Let's take a nap here. We'll need it."
"I hope I can sleep. I'm a bit worried about what comes next."
"It'll be hard, but don't worry too much. It's best to do nothing right now."

With this, Shajee lay down with his head on his pack, and quickly went to sleep. Popey wanted to do the same, but thought that a quick look at the task ahead might help calm him down. He edged over to the river, and looked at the place where the imposing structure met the water.

It was full of small holes, and below the dark waterline stain large parts were washed away completely. This surprised Popey, as he was used to the Giants and their magic being so very powerful. But the river was melting it away. Water alone was stronger still.

Popey smiled at this thought, and then realized the stones might be ready to fall down at any moment. But as he thought it through, he saw that it took time to wear it down, and there was still so much stone left. It stood, it will stand, but it is not forever. It isn't everything.

Sitting alone for the first time since he started his journey, Popey found himself thinking back to River Flats and the people he left behind. He wondered what Lilly and Emily were doing, how Misha was handling herself. Mostly, he missed Em far more than he thought he would. As he stared at the rock, the lapping of water started to sound like the voices he left behind. Altogether, they sounded like the murmur and bubble of the big crowd on that fateful day. And that is when it occurred to him.

The stone was like Rouger, and the water was like... like something that was always there, but easily ignored. Seeing it dissolve is inevitable, but it doesn't happen all at once. Even when challenged, Rouger had a few tricks up his sleeves. He didn't fall down, not all at once.

As Popey sat there, not doing anything, he slowly became more and more tired. It would all come in time, because water was so powerful. It was the water that made the whole valley, he reasoned. It was water that made all that fine stone the Giants were harvesting.

Slowly, his head nodded down as he felt for the first time that he wasn't such a small person after all. At least, no smaller than anyone else. Not even the Giants.

The roar of the Demons above woke him, and he realized it was dark. He found his way back to Shajee, and noticed he was still asleep. How could he sleep so soundly? But Popey soon found that his shuffling around stirred the dark shape, and Shajee sat up with the same wide grin he always had.

"Ready to go to the land of the Giants, kid?"
"I thought we were already in it?"
"Nah, this side isn't where they live. Just all the Demons."
"So there are more Giants where we are going?"
"You wanted to see the Giants, right, kid?"
"Um, yes, I did, but... I thought..."
"Eyes open?" That grin never quit.
Popey grinned back, "Eyes open!"

With that, Shajee got up and slung his pack on his shoulders. There was no sign he was tired, or that the pack held the incredible weight it had to hold. It was one fluid motion, as if he was excited to get going again.

"Up this way, kid, and we'll find the way over."
"So we just walk across?"
"You have a better way?"
"Well, no, but all those Demons..."
"Come on, I'll show you. There's a lot they just don't see."

They climbed up a steep hill, their breath heavy enough to nearly pull them by itself. The noise became louder and louder, but less even. It was possible to make out individual Demons more clearly as they whizzed by.

"Almost there. When we get to the top, stay to the right and walk quickly."
"We don't run?"
"Too long. They won't see us." Shajee anticipated the next question.
"Can I take a drink first?"
"Good idea, let's stop before we get going and get a drink."

Popey liked the idea that he had a good suggestion, even if it wasn't much of one. He held on to that simple idea to make himself more brave. He could do this, he could get across. The smallest thing can conquer the largest, given time and effort.

"OK, let's take a breather, kid."
"We're almost at the top?"
"Just about. I don't like to ever stop where they can see us."
"What if they do see us?"
"Well, they'll probably think we're gophers or something."
"I don't like being though of as a gopher!"
"Well, kid, it works to get across."

Popey stood there breathing hard, wondering just what was ahead of him. The feeling that the smallest, unseen thing will eventually beat a large barrier was bubbling up in him, just the way he decided to go out traveling in the first place. He saw his dream again, turning toward the dawn and walking off regardless of who called him back. It was then that he felt the wind on his cheek, as in his dream, another unseen and unending force. This time, he grinned to Shajee first.

"Well, I guess we should get going, then."
"Sure thing, kid. I'll lead the way."

From this point on, the roar of the Demons was too harsh to be able to talk. They would have to go in silence. Popey knew he'd have to have his own determination, and it was pounding strong with every heartbeat.

They reached the top of the hill, and were nearly blinded the steady stream of lights coming at them. Shajee shouted something, and made a big motion with his arm to come along. He was clearly trying to give Popey encouragement, without knowing it wasn't needed. The steady wind from the side and the gusts with each passing Demon stirred him up without scaring him at all. Some of the gusts were strong and threatened to push the pair over, but Popey stayed on his task. One foot in front of the other.

As they got to the top, the stone had a few breaks in it they needed to leap across. But once on the other side, it appeared smooth as far as they could see or imagine. The lights never stopped coming, but they always went by without a second thought. The small pair was indeed invisible, as no one bothered to see them. They could do whatever they wanted.

On and on they marched, staying close together and never slowing for a moment. Popey's determination kept him moving, as tired as he was. But it was different than the day he took his first steps. This time it wasn't just from the heart, but had all of his heart and arm and brain working together. And the terrible secret, that he could see the world even if it couldn't see him, kept a wide grin on his face that seemed to spread with every step. His pulse was fast and heavy, but he never noticed it. He almost thought he could fly over the river!

After a short while, Shajee looked back. In the endless stream of lights Popey caught a "thumbs up" sign from him, which showed he was happy to see that grin. Perhaps he even felt the determination radiating out of Popey like the dawn of his dream.

The lights and the roar were a constant annoyance, but easy to ignore after a while. It was like the first day on the path, just one foot after the other and never mind what was going on around you. There was time to be made, there was a destination ahead.

As time passed, and the journey became tiresome, Popey realized that he was crossing this great river without even being able to see it. The unseen force was below them, still moving and still making the valley. He felt strong and proud that he had conquered it so easily, and had learned to ignore it just like everyone else. And then, it occurred to him, that he was only kidding himself like all these Giants. It didn't matter what he thought; the river was always there, and always the great force.

After what would have been three or four handspans, if they weren't at night, the end of this thing was finally in sight. Popey was relieved, but also strangely sad. This part of the journey was over. A big goal had been reached. But like the river, Popey thought he was never really going to stop moving. He, too, was something of an unseen force.

When they reached the end of the stone, they slid down a hill just like the one on the other side. The lights stopped coming at them, and the dull roar of the Demons gradually faded. Popey and Shajee sat at the bottom of the hill and looked at each other. After not speaking for so long, they were almost out of practice.

"Well, kid, what'd you think?"
"Wasn't as bad as I thought!"
"You kidding me?"
"No, that was easy. Just keep walking, and they don't see you!"
"You're getting all brave again, are you?"
"Yes. Well, no, I just realized a few things, is all."
"Realized what?"
"That if you keep your eyes open, you're often the only one."
Shajee whistled, "Kid, that's the deepest thing you've said yet!"
"Well, it's true!"
"You bet it is!"
"You know what else I realized?"
"Tell me, you're on a roll."
"The smallest things no one sees can be the most powerful."
"Ah, there's the kid I picked up a few days ago."
"No, I mean it differently. It's not about force, it's about... about keeping at it and... well, about being there."

Shajee didn't say anything to this, but Popey couldn't help but think that he was being examined by an unspoken professor deep behind that grin. Popey wanted to tell him exactly what he meant, but now that the journey was over and the strange brew of determination had drained down it didn't seem as obvious. Besides, it wasn't that important to him to get Shajee's approval for all of these thoughts anymore.

"Nevermind. I was just looking at things for a while and noticed stuff."
"It's OK, kid. We're all tired, and we need to bed down in a safe place."
"Is this spot good?"
"It'll do well. A bit loud, though. Wanna go over there?"
"Down below?"
"Yeah, we can set up camp where we know we won't be seen. It'll be a lot more quiet."
"Sure."

They walked some distant downriver where it dropped down again, and soon the roar was only a thin whoosh. A clearing was found in the tall grass that looked flat and dry, but hidden. The pair of them quickly put a small frame shelter together, and soon they were asleep. There was nothing more to be done. They were safe, and on the other side.

Through the night, Popey dreamed over and over the same dream he had when he started. This time, no one called his name. The gentle breeze from before had also become the gusts of the passing Demons on the crossing. The waving whistle of the cordgrass had become the sound of his own feet. But the rest of it was the same. Popey slept hard, despite dreaming so heavily, exhausted from the path behind him.

CHAPTER 11:
PEOPLE OF POWER

They woke up late, sleeping well past dawn. Popey hadn't slept this late since… he had to think a while, and remembered sleeping in the day the Demon destroyed his home. He had worked into the night before that day, too, trying to get enough together to buy a nicer place to live. It was hard to make sense of everything that happened since. He opened his eyes slowly, trying to make sense of what he saw around himself now.

Shajee wasn't stirring at all, so Popey crawled out of the hastily made shelter and went to see the day on his own. He was hungry, and nibbled on one of the seeds he still had in his pockets. There weren't many left. He stood there, hidden as a part of the cordgrass patch, eating carefully as though it was his very last seed. The sun warmed him, and the breeze made a gentle whistle through the grass. Suddenly, he heard something more over the rustle and whoosh.

"Shajee, wake up! I hear voices!"
"Wha? What's up?"
"I heard voices, over there!"
"Lemee see what we got."

Shajee was up in a second, leaving his heavy pack behind but not out of arm's reach. He stood at full attention, listening, for just a few moments before his grin spread back over his face.

"We got Travelers, kid! There's a camp just over there!" He pointed quickly, then waved his hand over to grab his pack.
"Travelers? Other people on the path?"
"Sure, kid. This is where a lot of paths come together. Follow me!"

They ran off towards the voices without breaking their camp, eager to meet someone else after so many days walking alone. Shajee carried his pack in one arm, too excited to bother to fling it onto his back. Popey stayed back a strong half step, not exactly sure who or what they were about to see. After tramping through thick cordgrass for a short while, the stalks started to thin. And in another clearing were two Hopnegs, squatting down on the ground with blankets in front of them.

"Tenk! Jongo! How are you guys?" Shajee shouted.
"Shajee, hey! Long time no see." "What's up big guy?" They shouted back.

Popey saw their expressions change from very serious to open and friendly when they saw Shajee. They were both older, and much better dressed. One wore a very fine blue cloak over a white silk shirt and dark blue pants. The other had a long black coat that was open at the top, revealing a lavender shirt and red tie. They each had jewels all over them, their wealth obvious in harsh glints of sunlight.

Shajee dumped his pack down, and in one well rehearsed motion removed a blanket, spread it out in front of him, and started taking things out of the pack Popey never knew were in there. All kinds of household appliances, musical instruments, and other gadgets were spread out and displayed. The whole time, Shajee was unusually chatty about his stuff.

"These here all came from River Flats, they're all fleeing these days. I got some reasonable deals, but those townies are a lot more shrewd than you might think, so I can't give you any bargains. All the same, it's good quality stuff, they weren't any slouches, and I'm sure you'll agree some of this is top-shelf, like this flute..."

He was interrupted quickly: "Who is that punk?" It was the one with the blue cloak, who scowled like he just eaten a chokecherry. "Him? Oh, he's from River Flats. He's a good kid."

Popey stopped listening. He was so angry the sound of blood pounding in his ears made it impossible to hear. Who was this guy, calling him a punk? He tramped back into the grass, avoiding some bad words he'd rather not say, and plopped down. He sat there a long while, breathing hard, when finally Shajee found him again.

"Hey, kid, sorry about that. I did get some good trades with them, though."

"Who were those guys?"

"Just other Travelers. No one important."

"They why do they act and dress like bigshots?"

"Because they can? I don't know, kid. People do that."

"So they aren't rich and powerful?"

"Not really. They're just Travelers, making camp at the end of the day like anyone else."

If this was supposed to make Popey feel less mad, it wasn't. If these guys were the same as anyone else, then they had no right to act that way. Besides, even people with real power didn't have a right to act that way. All this talk and dress-up was just a show, a big fake show. He looked at his own filthy pajamas under his simple green coat. It was enough for him.

When Popey looked up, Shajee had a wrinkle of worry across his face. But Popey smiled at him quickly and deeply.

"It's allright. They don't bother me. I'm glad I didn't say what I was thinking!"

"Good for you, kid. I did learn a few things from them, though."

"Like what?"

"One of the places we find a lot of stuff has had a lot of Giants going through lately, dropping things. It's worth a side trip to check out."

"Well, ah, OK. But I'm more interested in getting downriver."

"Kid, this won't hurt. You'll see some stuff, maybe pick up the scratch to get you some supplies."

"Allright."

Popey suddenly felt a need to never have much of anything in his life, if all it did was make you into a jerk. 'All those fancy clothes, what do they do but wear out? Then, you've gotta get new ones.' He almost said what he was thinking out loud, but kept it in his head. Somehow, seeing Shajee nearly bow in front of those guys in order to make some money made Popey a lot quieter.

"We need some food, kid, aren't you hungry?"

"I guess I forgot in all the excitement."

"Let's eat up and spend a day relaxing here."
"Actually, Shajee, I'd like to eat and get going."
"You sure? You're not tired after all that?"
"No, I'd rather keep going now. Thanks."

They made their way back to the clearing they bedded down in, and soon had a fire going for the big meal. Popey wondered if he would ever get sick of this porridge, but it always warmed him deep down. By the time it was ready, he was very hungry and ate it quickly. When they both were finished, they sat back under the shelter for a while and said nothing. Eventually, Popey spoke up.

"Where are we going today?"
"Depends how far we can get, kid. It's tricky."
"Eyes open?"
"Yup, and I'm afraid mouth shut, too. Can't be seen or heard."
"I'll be as quiet as a houseguest."
"That's a saying I haven't heard in a while."

Popey smiled. He was thinking about the old ways again, what it was like before the Giants arrived. Somehow, that one bubbled up and came out like a deep spring that melts the ice around it. It just worked. He stared blankly for a moment thinking about everything he had seen so far. And there was still more to come.

"Well, kid, might as well."
"Sure, let's get at it."

The pack flung on and the shelter wrecked, all in one swoop, they were ready to go. In a moment, they were out of the cordgrass and into the open. That was when Shajee told him just how difficult their "side trip" was going to be.

"Allright then, we're off up the side of that big hill there."
"This one, where we came from?"
"No, to the right of it. The big one. All the way to the top."
"Up there? What's up there?"
"It's nice, but more to it that's the way to the good stuff."

Popey felt he was being misled, agreeing to this without seeing how hard it was. But when a breeze caught his cheek, he realized that he came this far with no idea what he was getting into. Like the wind, all he wanted to do was to keep going.

"How do we get up? It gets pretty steep."
"Yeah, well, you ever climb with ropes?"
"No, I'm from flatlands. Isn't that dangerous?"
"Nah, I'll show you. Besides, it's not all that steep."

For many handspans they clung to the rocks, usually tied together with a long rope that was apparently buried deep in Shajee's pack. He was ready for anything. But Popey wasn't ready for all this, and they were so heavily exposed on the side of the steep hill that silence really was essential. They couldn't call any more attention to themselves if they were going to make it through. The heat and effort beat them back, but they kept going. Higher, and higher. If it wasn't for the breeze on his back, Popey would have given up.

Finally, they reached the top. Popey's leg was shaking now that he allowed his fear to get the best of him, and had trouble with the final lift over the edge. With all the strength he had, he pulled himself up and over in a roll that was hardly elegant.

"Here, kid... have a drink." Shajee seemed a bit worried.
"Thanks."

From the top, Popey sat and sucked in as much air as he could, then as much water as he could from the canteen. Up here, he could see the whole valley – and where they came from as well. It was simply breathtaking in the size and all the colors and textures. The fat muddy water came into it from who knows where, and kept going on beyond. It was the one constant, and Popey found himself deeply admiring it.

He was absolutely empty from the climb, so there was nothing he could do but enjoy the view. And he had spent so much time in that valley, and used up so much of his strength climbing out of it, that he felt like it was a part of him now.

"Let's... rest a while, kid."
"Yeah... stop a bit... that's where... we were..."
"You can see River Flats... it's off over there... somewhere."

"Where we... crossed... it seems so small."

Shajee was finally sure that his companion was OK, so he said nothing. They both panted out their exhaustion there on the edge, not having the strength yet to leave this great valley behind them.

Popey couldn't help but notice how little the work of the Giants stood out when you got that far up and back. Yes, there was the crossing, and he could see that awful place where the rocks were harvested. But so much of it was the tall cottonwoods that might as well be grasses from up here. He then thought of the long walk, and how so much of it was spent under the trees. Of course the Giants weren't that big a part of the journey, he saw that. But what he remembered was a little different – until now. Now that he was exhausted, and now that he felt like one with the valley, and saw what it really was – scarred, but not destroyed.

Popey smiled broadly and thought again of the old ways, what it was like before the Giants arrived. For the first time in his life, he could imagine those days. And he could imagine what kind of magic there was deep in these woods, drifting along in the breeze. That was how Popey finally caught his breath.

"I've never been at the top of the valley before."
"It is something, isn't it, kid?"
"Just... incredible, really."
"So what're you thinking about now?"
"Nothing, really. Nothing at all."
"You're not trying to figger it all out?" Shajee grinned at him.
"Should I?"
"You usually do. I thought this place'd get you going good on that."
"Nah, I'm not... I think I decided I'm never going to figure it all out."
"Good thinking, kid. None of us will, you know."

Popey stared out blankly again. He suddenly felt a lot more interested in keeping his eyes open than keeping his mind full. It was so beautiful, so obvious and yet so mysterious.

"I'm not worried about a lot of things anymore."

"Well, kid, we have some ground to make up today."
"I'm rested, if that's what you mean."
"I just didn't want to peel you away before you were ready."
"I'm ready."
You caught your breath?"
"As much as I need to catch it."
"Good. It's a good walk from here, now."

They stood up, and Shajee coiled his rope back up and stuffed it into his pack. He then flung it back on and started off in the direction of a grassy field that was only knee-high, but thick. In the distance, there were small stone mountains, or hills, that looked like the Giants had made them. Popey was a little nervous about this.

"Where are we?"
"This is where the Giants live, in those. Don't worry, we'll dodge 'em."

Shajee led them between some hills and over the thick field. Popey couldn't help but realize how, for all the grass they were passing, there was so little else that was alive and cheerful.

"What is this stuff? Why is it so short and broken?"
"I dunno, kid. The Giants seem to like it."
"Sure is quiet here. Do they like it this dead?"
"I guess. You're back to your old self, now!"
"Yeah, I'm a bit... freaked by this. It goes on so long, and so dead."
"That's the Giants for you, kid. They like things big."

That would make sense, being Giants. But there was more to it than that to Popey. His mind had suddenly switched on again, away from the edge, and wasn't going to turn off soon. He kept tramping through the grasses behind Shajee, not paying any attention to where they were going.

"It's more than that... it's bigger than them, bigger and bigger."
"Well, they always seem to want more, as you saw in your old place."
"Yeah. They took the land itself. But we're not like that."
"Who's we, kid?"
"Hopnegs. We aren't like that at all."

Shajee laughed hard, "I see you forgot Tank and Jongo already!"
"Oh, those guys."
"Yeah, they're brutal, I'll tell ya! Tough guys to make a deal with."

Popey thought about them for a while, and knew Shajee was right. They were all the same, everywhere. It was about how big you could do it up, how much you could get away with. The only thing he ever got away with was escaping death, and that seemed like enough to him. If only it was enough for everyone, he wouldn't be where he was right now. But he really enjoyed being out traveling, and decided that was just that – enough.

"I'm not like that, and I don't think you are, either."
"Kid, just cuz I'm nice doesn't mean I'm not like them, I mean, this way."
"You always want more?"
"Sure, kid. And you don't?"
"I think I want less, actually."
"Well, kid, that's always easy to get, I guess. If you really do want it, that is. Here it is, let's stop."

A small stream of very clear water ran on the edge of what seemed like a long tube, coming out of the mountain. Was it a spring of some kind? Whatever it was, the water was cold and clean and very good tasting. They dumped their canteens, and filled them again with this good water without saying a word. In a few moments, they were ready to go.

"Let's bed down there and take a quick nap, kid. We have another long evening ahead of us."
"We're going to go at night?"
"I don't want to be seen, so I think it's best.

They left the place where there was water, and found a spot more dry and cool. Shajee dropped his pack, and lay down on it quickly. Popey propped his canteen behind his head for his own pillow, and soon they were both asleep. The climb was enough for now. It all was much more than enough for Popey.

CHAPTER 12:
INSIGHT

This time, it was Shajee who woke up first. His voice softly but firmly rattled Popey's otherwise deep and quiet sleep.

"Kid, c'mon, wake up! I think we have something here!"
"Uh, wha? Huzzup?"
"I have an idea for a short-cut, you'll like this. Let's get on it."
"What... how long were we..."
"Just a short nap, really. It's still light, y'see."
"I thought... safer at night."
"This'll work, trust me. I saw where we are."

So Popey flipped himself up, dazed from the irregular sleep schedule they were suddenly keeping. It was good to have a nap, but traveling more right now seemed hard. Still, Shajee was so eager to get where they were going it made Popey confused and a little angry. What were they getting into?

"OK, Shajee, I'm ready to go now."
"Great, off this way and we'll be there."
"This place you want to go to?"
"No, the short-cut. Ah, we'll hitch a ride." He grinned almost dangerously.
"Hitch a ride?"
"It'll save us days of walking, you'll see."

With this, they set out. Popey was getting upset at not being told everything again, but it never turned out all that badly. It was just getting old, the same routine of being given a hint and no more. But it couldn't be any worse than climbing the mountain, he reasoned. Besides, on his own he would never have gotten this far.

"What is this place?"
"Well, kid, the oldsters told me this used to all be the Giants' farms."
"With all these mountains everywhere?"

99

"They came later, after the farms. Apparently, they didn't want to farm anymore."

"We had a Giant's farm next to us, but I never understood any of it."

"What do you mean, kid?"

"They had strange ways, like they do with everything I guess."

"I don't even try to understand them anymore, kid. I just deal with it."

Popey could relate to that after what he had been through. It made a lot more sense to just keep his eyes open and see. But that got him right back to something else bugging him.

"This ride we're going to get, what is it?"

"I can't explain, kid, you'll have to see. It's not as dangerous as it sounds."

"It's not the danger, it's... I like walking, is all."

"Save us days, kid, days of walking."

"I don't want a short-cut like that, is all."

"Try it once, then you tell me. Days of walking, I'm serious."

It was no use. He had his mind made up, and Popey had no other way to know where to go than to just follow. Patience kept him trudging along this far, but it was getting very thin. But Popey kept going back to how, for the first time in his life, being out walking gave him time to think.

"A few days and maybe I'd learn why this isn't a farm anymore."

"I suppose, kid, but I don't know that anyone else ever figured it out."

"It seems like good land, dark and spongy."

'You'd know, kid. I just go with what they do."

"We're going over there, to that place?"

"Yeah, you'll see when we get there we have some thing to avoid."

On they walked, and something like a lake came into view. But as they got closer, it wasn't blue but a dark black, with heat bubbling out of it and distorting everything around it. Maybe it wasn't a lake, but very rich dark earth? Popey had to ask.

"Is that bare earth up ahead?"

"No, kid, it's something else. I dunno, but stay away. Too hot to go near."

"So it's not rich soil, huh?"

"I'm sure nothing ever grew there, kid. We'll stay to this side and wait."

"For what?"

"For the light blue Demon that sometimes comes by."

"We're hitching a ride on a Demon?" Popey's eyes opened in alarm.

"Don't be afraid, it's safe enough."

"I've been on Demons before, I'm…. I can handle this."

"You have? Allright, kid, this won't be so bad as I thought."

When they got to the edge of the strange lake, they moved quickly towards the mountain at the side. There was shade there, and a chance for a short break while Shajee kept his attention towards the black spot. He spoke slowly as he fished into the bottom of his pack.

"OK, around this time of day you can see the light blue Demons with the white diamond on the side. They are going where we want. When we see it, we run to the back and you take the rope and when I say to get on my shoulders, you do it. Then, I'll toss you up into the hollow space and you lower the rope for me, got it?"

"You're kidding me, we jump up into it?"

"Sure, it's a rough ride, but nothing too bad. I know where they're going."

"And this beats walking to you?" Popey was a little mad.

"It's not like it's… Here's one! That's the one!"

Popey turned to see the Demon, just as described, stop with a lurch and a clatter. It was just like the one he was on before, out in the field, if just a shade smaller. It vibrated and whirred the same sort of way, and even though it was still for a moment it was very much alive.

"Here's the rope. Follow me, kid!"

They sprinted off to the back of the Demon, stopping only briefly to see if there were any Giants around. There were some, standing just a short distance away, but Shajee apparently decided they weren't looking their direction. When they got under the hot and loud Demon, it was time.

"On my shoulders, quick!" He was shouting over the deafening noise.
"Oof, OK, now what do I jump to?"
"See that hollow spot, runs the width."
"Got it!"
"Here we go then, 1, 2, 3!"

Popey found himself propelled up, and he landed in something like a cave that was large and flat. He had to scramble to get his legs in with the rest of him, and then turn around lying flat. In the noise and confusion, he almost forgot he had to lower the rope, but when he got his senses he dropped it quickly and held on to his end tightly.

"Here I come! Hold on tight!"

Shajee and his pack weighed even more than Popey thought, and he nearly slid back off the edge. Once again, it was his determination alone that got him through, and soon the grinning face peered over the edge. Shajee flipped himself over with surprising quickness, and landed with a hard thud that echoed the vibrations of the Demon. They were up! They were in the guts of the Demon!

"That was great, kid! I'm real glad I have you with me."
"What do we do now?" They were both shouting.
"Hold on tight. And let's not say anything, OK? They might hear us."
"Over this noise?"
"Making sure, kid."

They sat in silence a while, absorbing the nervous twitches of the Demon. Suddenly, the whole thing sank lower, and made a series of dull thuds. A quick moment later, and they were clearly moving forward. They were off, going somewhere in the belly of the Demon. Popey couldn't believe that they had actually gotten a ride on one of these! The clatter and pitch and roll kept his heart in his throat the whole time, but somehow he knew that he was not in any immediate danger. He wanted to ask Shajee some questions, but decided that silence would be the safest thing. He would have to just enjoy the ride.

It was not a long ride, but it seemed forever. The Demon stopped a number of times, and with each jerking halt Shajee would peer over the edge to look for something. Eventually, he peered over and turned to Popey with an eyebrow raised, and the Demon suddenly pitched back up again.

"We're here, kid! Can you jump?"
"Sure."
"Let's go!"

And with one quick hop, they were on the ground. It was hard, black and stony, with a greasy smell. Popey looked around a moment, and then stared hard at Shajee, who was doing the same.

"Over here, kid, let's run! First we'll hide and check it out."

They dropped into a narrow trench that seemed to give them some cover. It was as ugly and gray as the stone harvesting place, and just as spooky. Shajee looked around, and then silently pointed, touched his mouth to signal silence, and then waved Popey on. He understood. Shajee was out of the trench first, and then through the large opening with Popey close behind, at full run all the time. Past the opening, there was a dark corner to slip into, and they panted over to it in silence. There were inside… where?

"I think we can talk now, kid."
"Where are we? It's full of Giants!"
"Busy ones, aren't they?"
"Yes! What is this!"
"Keep your voice down. They go through here all the time, faster and faster. This is where we get the good stuff."
"Jewels? You take this risk for jewels?"
"You got it, kid."
"This is insane!"

They sat there a moment, thinking about where they were. Popey kept hearing a voice, off in the distance, that sounded urgent. He couldn't help but think that it was announcing their impending doom, the end of the world. Dozens and hundreds of Giants went past, many with fancy clothes and all carrying bags. They looked like Travelers, but they all kept moving without stopping to trade and tell stories. Colorless expressions hung loosely from every face. Perhaps they were too important to be friendly?

The floor they stood on was just as incredible, a highly polished stone of some kind. It was cold and slippery under Popeys hard feet, and felt like glass. This was the main Hall of the Giants, the Palace, or something like it, Popey reasoned. He asked Shajee what it was all about.

"What is this place, do you know?"
"Not really. But I can show you something that seems important."
"It's where we are going?"
"Yup. Need a break here to run over to that door. Might be coming."
"Run over there?"
"Yes... here it is... OK, go!"

They ran as fast as they could, not stopping as they went past a huge Giant door and into a different place, a place with differently polished floors that came in pieces with rough spots between. It smelled odd, and Popey thought he might gag on the harsh chemical smell. But Shajee waved him on, and in a moment they were by a small hole in the massive walls. Shajee dove in, and Popey went after. In the space that was about his size Popey felt safe for the first time since they got here.

"Where does this go?"
"We slide down from here. Ready?"

Shajee grabbed onto a metal tube as wide as his armspan, and waved Popey to follow. In a flash, he was gone, and Popey wearily did the same thing. Down they flew, until a sudden bend forced them to let go and drop. With a sharp thunk, they landed in a place as big as the Giants but much quieter than the place above.

"Here we are, kid!"
"Where is that?"

"The underside, the place where all those Giants leave stuff behind."

"What is this place?"

"Oh, yeah, look out there." Shajee pointed to a huge window. Popey quickly moved over to it to stare.

Just outside, there was a Demon like he never saw before – long and narrow, but with something like wings attached. It looked like a bird in flight, even on the ground. And then Popey saw one moving very fast, and leap into the air right in front of him.

"The Giants have flying Demons?"

"Apparently. This is the only place you see 'em, though."

"Doesn't this scare you?"

"Ha! Now you ask me! Well, it did at first, but you get used to it."

"They never see you?"

"No, they don't. From the look of 'em, they're too busy."

"And this is where the 'good stuff' is?"

"Right over here, follow me!"

Popey was very nervous about all of this, but tramped along behind as usual. It was so bright in here, yet so gray, and so easy to be seen. At least there were no Giants down here in this place! They kept moving for a very long time, not saying a word, when finally Shajee stopped.

"I think this is it, kid! This is the stuff I was told about!"

He pointed out in front of them, to a big pile of gray and metal and a few shiny things as well. Yes, there were a few jewels hidden in what appeared to be a sort of trash pile. But what kind of trash was it?

"I don't understand. Is this what they throw out?"

"They keep adding more things to this place, and that's when you get good stuff."

"It's still being built?"

"Yeah, sort of. Look at this!" He held up a rough shiny piece that was a brilliant red, a deep color that shown even though it was uncut to be a jewel.

"They keep building this… this palace? And throw all this away?"

"Yup, look at it all! You load up those empty pockets, too. You'll need it."

Shajee had his pack out, and was stuffing it with everything shiny that he could find – metal, rough jewels, everything. Popey grabbed what he could as well, and in just a short time they each had all they could carry. They were both covered in the thin gray dust that made up most of the pile by the time they were done, but Shajee's grin shown through it.

"This is the big load, kid. Between this and what I got before, I'm going to finally be a wealthy man!"

"That's good, Shajee. But what do we do with this uncut stuff?"

"Oh, you'll see, real shortly. There's another town here where they take care of all that."

"Piketown? It's here?"

"Yup, kid, you got it. Piketown. We'll be there soon."

"Well, I would like to get out of here. I'm so sleepy, even if it is daytime."

"Oh, it's well into the night. These lights are on all the time, it's dark outside."

With that, Shajee pointed out the window again. Sure enough, it was dark outside – but with lights that lit up everything, everywhere. Popey was horrified to realize that his whole sense of time had been upset by this place, and with it his whole sense of where he was in the world. He blushed again, thinking he had just committed some terrible crime.

"You OK, kid?"

"Yeah, I'm OK. I was just… thinking about all those busy, important looking Giants. What's this place all about?"

"I can't say, kid. They seem to have so much they don't mind dropping a bunch for us. So I can't say I mind it a bit!"

"Don't you feel like a thief? Don't they look like thieves, having all that?"

"I don't know what you mean."

"Where does it come from? Who's was it?"

Shajee thumped his pack. "It's mine now!"

Popey was silent for a while, and realized that with his sense of time shot he totally forgot to have dinner. He was hungry.

"Is there some place we can prepare a meal here?"
"There's plenty of food, back up where they run around. Follow me, I'm hungry, too."

They found their way to what seemed to be an enormous moving staircase, and when it was clear no one was around they got on it, and went up. Popey was trying to dust himself off the whole time, convinced that the gray was some kind of mark of his crime. Nothing here was any good, none of it was what he wanted. He was ashamed and tired and hungry and just a little bit angry. But he also knew he was a lot richer, if only he could convert these things in his pockets into something useful.

After scampering and dodging and a few full-out runs, the pair made their way to a place where the busy Giants seemed to stop and linger. There were sweet and salty and sour smells, and quite a few good things to eat just lying on the ground. They hauled a big piece of what appeared to be bread over to a corner, and ate greedily. They stayed silent, out of fear of being discovered, but Shajee whispered over to his companion in pride.

"Quite the place, isn't it, kid?"
"All these important Giants with so much stuff! And it's never dark!"
"And they drop such wonderful things. It's the life!"
"If you don't mind living like a deermouse!"

They finished the rest of their meal in silence.

Chapter 13:
Easy by Nature

When they were done eating, Popey wanted nothing more than to get out of that place. He told Shajee this quickly and quietly, and with a nod the two set off to the same slide they used before. The constant activity had thinned, but never stopped. Popey realized it must be the middle of the night, but still the Giants crossed the polished floor with their huge bags behind.

The tiny pair scampered off to the slide down below, and dropped down as before. No one seemed to notice or care, and Popey started to feel like he was invisible. Or did they see, but not take notice because he was a punk? Popey smiled at the thought that there might be a real use to being a punk after all. The lowest of them all are the most invisible, he figured. And here they were, back down below all that action, once again. From this place, there was no competition with the blur of gray Giants.

"Where to now, Shajee? Is there a quick way out?"
"There is, kid. I think it's... yeah, it's this way."

Off they went, a different way than to the trash pile of great wealth. This time, Popey started to smell the clear air and a hint of something oily. The noise from – the birds? – came up once in a while, scaring him on quicker. Eventually, a huge opening gave them passage to the outside. It was good to be out, but they still were in a terrible place. It was deafeningly loud, all the time, and the smells were so oily and hot and wrenching.

"I think it's... sure, kid, follow me. We got it!"
"Where are... we going?"
"The fast way down. We need... here, take this."

With that, Shajee hoisted over a very large, white container that was much bigger than both of them. It had two parts to it, and once Popey grabbed the other end he found it was surprisingly light. He held onto it, not sure what was happening, when Shajee started cutting the two parts down the middle with his pack saw. Popey was very confused.

"What is this?"
"Trash, I guess. Hold it up a bit, like that, now up and down."
"Where did it come from?"

Shajee was halfway through, and stopped a moment as if to rest. He looked over the half they were going to use.

"Well, it says something on it. S-Z-E-C-H and then C-H-I-C-K. I don't know what those mean, kid."
"Some kind of magic?"
"It could be, I dunno."

With that, Shajee got back to work, and soon he was done. Once the halves were separated, Shajee quickly flung the one end that was cleaner down into a big hole in the ground and watched it disappear.

"Why'd you do that, Shajee?"
"Follow me, we're behind it!"

With that, Shajee tied a rope carefully to the slats of the huge metal floor they were standing on , and dropped it down. Shajee crawled down the rope, and Popey simply did the same thing behind him without thinking. It was good to get out of this place. In a short while, they reached the bottom where the white half-container lay in near darkness, and Shajee yanked at the rope.

"Gotta... c'mon... get loose, you can... Here we go!" In several jerks, the rope finally was free and fell beside them both. Shajee coiled it, much less frantic than he was on the top, and obviously catching his breath a bit.

"Flip that over, and set it on the edge of that tube, there."
"Over here?"
"Yeah, there. I'll be there soon." It was a thin trickle of water that showed the way.
"We're going down the tube?"

"It'll be quite a ride, so hold on." Shajee hopped in with this, and went to the front. "Kid, when we both lean forward, it'll move. Then, you can pull back and keep it from going too fast. This'll be a ride, but you hold on!"

"OK, I'm ready." Popey wasn't really ready, but he did want to move.

"Forward, now!" Shajee slammed himself into the sloping front side.

With that, they lurched forward just a little, and then came the slithering feeling that they were moving. And it got faster. And faster. Sliding, scraping along the bottom with the sound of a very angry snake fast behind them. Sprays of water in their faces kept showing them the way. It was totally dark and nothing hit their senses except the noise and the excited stream. Screaming fast, then bottomed out a moment in a flat place, and then screaming again. Popey lost any thoughts of anything else for a while.

This kept on, sliding down the tube, and gradually Popey felt a strange warmth inside of him. He was moving down, like water, always down. He knew they'd be in the river bottom area again, for the first time since they looked out over it. He liked that idea. And since he was going some place he loved and knew, Popey found himself not worried about the noise or the dark. In fact, he almost thought he could see the tube, lit up around them from a light that came from deep within him. He wasn't afraid, he knew what he was doing. Adventure only made his blood run hotter now, and kept his face warm despite being very wet. This was a good feeling. This was the fire inside of him.

Popey smiled broadly and let the warmth stream behind him. Just a few bumps and flat sections interrupted the constant wail and downward plunge. Suddenly, just as he was completely relaxed, it happened: with a hard splat that sent his jaw into his skull there was silence. Everything had stopped.

"Whew! You OK, kid?"
"Yeah… where are we?"
"Great ride, wasn't it? We're here, or almost here."
Popey realized they were floating. "Are we in the river?"

"Naw, just a pond. Can you reach down and paddle... over there?"
"Sure."

Soon, they were both drenched in their effort to lean over and paddle their strange boat to the shore. It took a long time, since progress was slow, but soon enough they bumped up against the shoreline. It was hard to see anything in the light they had, but Shajee was confident as always.

"Here we go, kid. Great ride, wasn't it!"
"Yeah, are we in the river bottom?"
"Sure are. Let's make camp right here."
"I'm totally wiped, I could use a long sleep."

With that, they both hopped out of the boat. Popey went first, and held on as the much heavier Shajee and his pack pushed out. They found a few twigs and taller grasses, made their shelter fast, and crawled inside.

"Kid, aren't you cold? You're wetter than I am!"
"I'm kinda wet, Shajee. But I'm allright."
"Let's start a fire, we can do that here and be safe."

With that, they climbed out and gathered a few twigs. In a moment, they had a great big fire going and were back under their cover. Shajee was asleep in a moment, his clothes softly steaming as the wet boiled off into the thick night air. Popey couldn't help but think he didn't need a fire, even as the reflection of it out in the pond lulled him to sleep. He was still very warm inside.

Again, they slept until the sun was several handspans high. Popey woke up restless and still tired. It was good to sleep in, but it hardly helped. He stirred the embers and threw some grass on, and soon it was roaring again. Popey stared blankly at it, absorbing the heat. Shajee stirred, and sat up quickly.

"You hungry, kid?"
"Yeah, very."

Without saying another word, Shajee started making a fresh batch of porridge for breakfast. Popey stared out at the pond and the bottomland he had learned to love. Beyond the fire that was so close, by a small stand of grasses that swayed in the wind, a wood duck whistled. And everything was wet, everywhere he looked. He smiled at how water pointed the way, and how it settled in the lowest places. This was what he remembered as home. After all the work on the porridge was done, and it was just a matter of simmering, Shajee spoke.

"Today we'll get into Piketown, kid. You'll like it."
"I can't wait! But I have to say I'm not thrilled about towns anymore."
"Yeah, townies can be all messed up in the head. But this place is different."
"I hope so. It's such a legend."
"As it should be, kid! It's the end of the path, you know. The far end of the world for us. OK, I think she's done, here."

They took their time eating, slurping down each mouthful carefully as if not wanting to disturb the peaceful, damp air. Eventually, Popey felt he had to say something.

"You know, it's amazing how beautiful it is here, down so low."
"Well, kid, you like this a lot better than the bluff edge, I can tell."
"It's so... you just follow the water down. It's a forgotten, unwanted place. That's what makes is special, I guess."
"You're getting deep again, kid. Deep! Ha! Didn't mean to joke, there."

They said little more until they were done, and quickly wrecked their shelter and packed up. Shajee pointed, "This way, follow me, it's a few handspans from here," and off they went. The way was hot, but peaceful, and alive with small animals and bugs. Every now and then, a dragonfly would hover just beyond them, as if it wondered where they were going. Popey smiled at each one like a friend.

Soon, they came to another stone part of the path, much smaller than the big one they crossed before. Popey stopped even before

Shajee when he saw how open and visible it was, which caused Shajee to stop short of the edge he wanted to peer out over.

"It's OK, kid. There's hardly no Giants here at'all."
"We're crossing that, Shajee? Where does it go?"
"It's an island, it's Piketown. Just another handspan from here."
"It's awfully out in the open."
"They don't mind." And Shajee pointed to a group of three Travelers, their packs swaying as their long coats swished, marching along the path. The sight of more Hopnegs made Popey both happy and anxious. They were near their goal, but the goal itself wasn't obvious.

"OK, Shajee, I'm with you. Let's go." Popey made himself brave. There was no time like the present to just do it, to act and get this done.

They hiked along over flat, level ground for quite a while, through a place thick with brush. It was the well-beaten path that let them know where they were with no good landmarks. And then, the brush cleared, and a row of small wooden homes appeared with dust and smoke coiling up into the sky. A gentle patter of Hopneg activity lit the air. Piketown. It was here.

"Well, kid, first things first, I guess. You seen yourself lately?"
"No, I haven't. Am I dirty?"
"Dirty? Ha! You're a mess! We need to stop by this well and clean up."

Sure enough, just beyond the edge of the clearing, was a small well. It may have been just for Travelers. Shajee pulled out a shiny piece of metal and held it up to Popey so that he could see. The image was strange and horrible. His hair was matted, and was that a beard he had started? It was like he had aged years. They both cleaned up, Popey taking a lot of time to scrub off the mess of the paths they had been on. Then, with a nod, Shajee started out again to the buildings.

"Now, we have to get us a little something from all this treasure, kid."
"What do you mean?"

"Get some jewels made. You'll see."

"I still have my eyes open, yes!"

"Oh, you don't have to here, kid! It's a busy place, but it's OK."

"But I want to see it all!"

"Oh… sure, kid, I remember my first time here!" Shajee laughed heavily.

As they walked along, all kinds of Hopnegs passed by, busy with something. None of them seemed to look at the pair, as if they were still invisible. Popey noticed that the level ground was perfect for their buildings of sticks, which had an amazing air of permanence to them. Everything was straight and even, and made to last. And everything seemed to be ordered and peaceful, as if ruled by a very powerful Hopneg.

"Shajee, who runs this place?"

"Well, kid, it's a Council of elders and stuff. I don't really understand it."

"There's no single elder who is in charge?"

"No, it's… it's complicated. They have their own ways, here."

"It's so clean and orderly."

"Yeah, it's not the wild place you thought. Well ... here we are, in here."

Shajee led the way into a shop with the title "Jeweler" on the door in careful black and gold letters, and the name "Elada" below that. Inside it was well lit with lamps, and a middle-aged woman with beautiful eyes, a rounded nose, and curly blonde hair stood behind a counter. She wore a green dress of very fine cloth, and a gentle lace edged collar that rose above it to kiss her hair. Everything about her looked serene and friendly.

"Shajee!" She shouted, "Where have you been!"

"Elada, my love! I have been so many places. But I always wanted to be with you! Oh, this is Popey, he's from Riverflats." Shajee bowed slightly.

"How do you do? I'm sorry about your town. Are you seeking refuge?" Elada was as kind as she looked.

"Um, no." Popey fumbled, unsure what to say. "I'm just Traveling."

"My dear, we have some business you may be interested in." Shajee was acting a lot more like he did with the other Travelers before.

Elada giggled in a way that popped her serenity like a balloon. "Stop it, Shajee, I can see you were up there by that gray grime still on you! Let's go to the shop and show me what you found."

She let them through a door into a large yet cramped room, full of benches and boxes. The ceiling hung low like a weight on their shoulders, and the lighting was not as good. Shajee immediately emptied his pockets of all the sparkling things they had collected, and Popey did the same after him. Shajee was suddenly animated by the sight of it all.

"See this one I think is especially good, you'll get a lot from that one! I'm all out since I traded for the goods in Riverflats, so I need a little something to get me started, we can get the rest later. Now this one is..."
"Shajee, dear," Elada interrupted him, "You don't have to." She smiled at him coyly. "It wouldn't work on me anyways. I know you."

With a wink, Elada picked up one of the long ruby colored hunks of something like glass from Popey's pile. Holding it to the light streaming in the window ahead of her, she rolled and turned it in her hands, silencing the room in a dazzle of red light. Finally, she spoke to them, "They are so beautiful uncut. Each is unique. I hate to cut them... but it is what people want."

She placed the large shard down, and stared again as she reached for a hammer and tiny chisel. Elada held the chisel over the piece for a long time, as if the right moment to strike was as important as the right place. Then, when the timing was perfect, she acted. Crack! With a tiny noise that grew to fill the whole room, the first blow was set. Soon, it was followed by hundreds more, hammering and hacking away. And then, Elada stopped, grabbed the piece below her, and held it up.

"This is a good one, for sure. I can get twelve like this from this piece. I'll give you ten. What do you say... Popey, is it?"
"Um, yeah" Popey was fumbling again. Shajee elbowed him, "Take it!" Popey was unsure what was going on, but decided to speak with authority. "Yes, I'll take it. Ah, thank you!"

Shajee took over, now that Popey did what he had to. "Could you get this done now? He needs it right away, and I'll need some as well." Elada nodded. "I'll be happy to help you, you know that. I can get some done now, and have the rest by tomorrow. This is quite a haul, though. I will be a bit busy!" Shajee looked her over, slightly upset. "Does this mean you won't have time to see me tonight?" Elada kissed him on the cheek, and said, "No, I won't. But you have a date with a bathtub, instead!" She giggled again, and soon went to work.

Popey could not help but admire her skill. In a short time, she had six incredible ruby jewels to present to Popey. "Here are yours, young man, I hope you like them. This kind of wealth does not come every day. Now, Shajee, which do you want first?" Popey interrupted the two of them without thinking, transfixed by the pile in his hand. "Shajee, don't worry. I want you to have these two. From... from the bottom of my heart, I appreciate all you've done for me." Shajee was stunned. "Kid, you don't have to... I mean, thank you, but you don't..." Popey was sure of himself. "Take them, let's go wash up. Elada's right, we're still a mess."

Shajee snatched the jewels and said, "Thank you, Popey, you are very kind. Tonight, we sleep in a hotel. We're all rich!"
"A hotel?"
"I know a great one, just across the street, really."
"That would be nice.
"You don't know the half of it!" Shajee was grinning even more than he ever did before, if that was possible. "But first, I'd like to have a quick word with this lovely woman alone, if you don't mind."
"Ah, sure, you want me to go out to ... the store?"
"Thank you, Popey, I won't be long."

Popey went back to the first room they came into, filled with display cases, and closed the door behind him. There were so many things sparkling in the rich light he found himself stunned into being more tired than he had felt in a long time. He sank into a very comfortable chair by the door, and let it all wrap around him. All these jewels! Some were going to be his. He was rich? What did that mean? He never expected to be rich one day.

A short while later, the door startled open, and ended that thought. It was time to follow Shajee again, to find this hotel. The idea was exciting and warm. Shajee spoke in a calm and serious way that wasn't typical.

"Elada, I'll see to it. Don't worry, and we'll be back in the afternoon."
Elada paused a moment, and tossed her hair gently. "You do that. I can't wait to see you properly cleaned up!"
"Yes, my dear!" and Shajee bowed as elegantly as his large body could imagine with that pack still glued onto him.

With that, they said their goodbyes and left Elada to go to work. Shajee led the way to a large building labeled "Hotel Mitterer" and led inside. Popey hardly noticed what a clean, well lit and huge place it really was.

Mitterer was there to greet them, a young but balding Hopneg wearing a simple white shirt. He was kind, but businesslike. When Popey fumbled in his pocket for a jewel, and pulled out three together, Mitterer's eyes lit up briefly, the only real change in his expression the whole time. They each got a room, and some coins in change for one of the large red jewels, and Popey wandered off to his bed. Bed, and sleep. The tub would wait for tomorrow. He finished the last of his seeds, drank his canteen all the way down, and sank deep into the soft bed. Deeper yet came his sleep.

CHAPTER 14:
PARADOXES

Popey woke up early and fast, stretching his body into a warm patch of sun that leaked through the window. He was refreshed, and felt an urge to scrape the dirt off and feel clean.

He wandered into the bathroom that was attached to his room, and stared at the tub. This was nicer than anything he'd ever seen. The stove next to it had no hot water ready, but the pump on the other side showed water was easily available. He fiddled with the pump, and saw that it really worked. He started by stripping down and throwing his unbelievably dirty clothes into the tub, and then pumped enough water in to get them all wet. He then filled the large basin on the stove, lit the stove, and went to work.

Scrubbing his clothes took a long time, even with the large bar of soap and the brush the hotel thoughtfully provided. When he was satisfied, he emptied the tub with its own built-in drain, and rinsed his clothes out with more water. When they wrung out and hanging on the nearby hooks to dry, he dumped the water off the stove and into the tub. It was nice and warm, and would make for a great bath.

Popey must have spent a full handspan in the tub, just relaxing. Is this what it was like to be rich? Certainly, Rouger never looked dirty, or betrayed the smell of work. It felt so very good after his days traveling to feel this way.

Finally, he got out, dried himself with a towel, and combed his hair slick back. Everything he needed was right here, he thought. The deep mud of the tub water reminded him of the river that must be just outside this hotel. Popey watched it all swirl away with a sense of awe. He felt his clothes, which were still damp, but wearable. Before he slipped them on, he noticed that his pajamas didn't really come clean, but he smiled at the idea that some of the path was stuck to him forever.

He was unsure what to do next, so he made his bed up neat and tidy. He lay down on it to try to think, but found himself strung out and not able to concentrate. For one thing, he was hungry. Just as he was thinking about what would be next, there was a knock at the door.

"Um, come in?"
"Hey, kid, you allright in here?" The large figure, without his pack, nearly burst into the room. He was clean and his beard cut and almost... handsome?
"Yeah, I'm... I'm hungry, is all."
"Kid, you cleaned up good! Yeah, let's get breakfast."
"Where do we do that? On the stove?"
"No, you don't... it comes with the room! C'mon."

With that, Popey followed Shajee once again, this time through the long hallway and out to the main lobby. Popey realized he must have gone down the same way last night, but he was so tired then that he didn't remember it at all. When the way opened up into a large room, there before him was the biggest display of food he'd ever seen.

"Well, kid, have at it!"
"This is all for us?"
"Us, all the guests. Like I said, you paid for it!"

Popey followed Shajee's lead by picking up a plate and digging into the assortment of seeds and breads and meats in front of him. He had never seen anything like this before, ever, and his eyes must have showed it. When Shajee sat at a table with real chairs and a tablecloth, Popey slowly lowered himself across from him.

"It's OK, kid, this is what it's like for us now that we're rich!"
"All of this... stuff... and the bath..."
"Yeah, you know, you could have sent those clothes out to be cleaned. Or got new ones." Shajee stabbed at some meat with a fork and waved it around to punctuate the last thought.
"Oh, this, well... I'm fine this way, thanks."
"Suit yourself. Say, a suit... naw, ig wan gi'ar fance" The last thought was drowned out by chewing.
"Where is your pack, Shajee?"

"It's safe in the room. Mitterer runs a good place here."

As if he heard his name, the graceful figure of Mitterer loomed up to their table. He was still dressed in a white shirt and black pants, but now had added a simple black tie to the top.

"Good morning, gentlemen," he spoke cautiously, "I hope everything is to your satisfaction?"

"Yes, it is, thank you!" Shajee dabbed his lip with a napkin.

"And you, young man, is there anything I can do for you?" Mitterer seemed to be speaking purposefully.

"No, sir. I'm fine here." Popey felt out of sorts.

"We are hosting a bit of a... gathering tonight, if you gentlemen would like to come and join us."

"A party!" Shajee was excited now, "Sure, that would be great!"

Mitterer's glance was still on Popey, however. "Yes, I'm sure a young man like yourself could meet some people who could help him, if he so chose."

Popey was confused by being called 'he'. "Help him do what?"

Mitterer knelt down beside him and talked in more of a whisper. "I recognized Elada's fine work last night, and she spoke very highly of you, Popey." Popey was confused by this, and looked to Shajee for an explanation. All he got back was a wink and a grin. With nothing more in his brain than confusion, Popey sat silent for a while to see what would come next. Mitterer continued, "As it says in The Book, 'Reputation leads, wealth follows', and I can see that your reputation is deserved, young man."

Popey felt all morning that this was a different world, but now he was sure of it. It was a drop of water off his green coat hitting his ankle that finally spurred him to speak.

"You follow The Book here, too?"

"Of course we do. You are familiar with it?"

"Only in... well, a little." Popey blushed out the last words.

"Excellent. There is an opening for a Page here, serving the Council. It would give you time to learn all that you need to. I am certain that you can... afford it."

Popey was confused. "Afford it? What is this... you buy?"

"All of our Councilors start as Pages. When you… pay your consideration to the Council, you are really setting yourself up for a very good life."

Popey wanted Shajee to help him, but it was clear that Shajee was leaning back and away, trying hard to not pay attention. Popey thought about all the hard work he had known so far, and the offer was tempting. This life was certainly easier. But was it?

"Ah, thank you, Mitterer, I'll be here tonight."
"Excellent!" Mitterer rose, satisfied he had done his part. "I will see you then at sunset?"
"Ah, yeah, I guess… sunset, we'll be here."

As Mitterer left the table, Popey sat silent. Shajee felt as though he had to break the awkward silence that was now sitting on the table between them.

"Kid, this is a great opportunity! And just one day in town!"
"I dunno… Shajee, it sounds great, but…" Popey trailed off.
"No more heavy lifting, kid. Think about it."
"I was thinking that… I mean… to do it right is to bear everyone else's burden, to bear a lot of small… evils."
"What do you mean, kid?"

Popey stopped for a moment, and toyed with his food. He wasn't hungry anymore. Something was wrenching his guts too tightly.
"It's that I've seen this sort of… this being the leader and all, and it just doesn't seem… I dunno, right. There are so many things you have to do if you…" He trailed again, and then got his voice free from the twist in his guts. "It's that to be a leader, you have to have your heart and arm and brain in it, and not just read from some stupid book!"

Shajee was stunned for a moment, but gradually the grin came back over him, spreading slowly and deliberately above his now neatly trimmed beard. "I knew you had it in you, kid!"
"Is Piketown really different? Would people here understand this?"
Popey was in charge now, pulling the situation over to himself. He wasn't sure he liked the feeling.

"They follow The Book, if that's what you mean, kid. Whether they want or can handle more than that, I dunno. You'll have to see for yourself."

"Um." That wasn't the answer Popey wanted.

"Let's finish up and see some people. Friends of mine."

They quickly finished what was on their plates, and ducked out onto the dusty street. The light and bustling noise grabbed Popey's attention, stirring it up with the dust all around him. He paused just outside the hotel, and Shajee stopped to see what was the matter.

"Kid, you allright?"

"Yeah, I just was wondering. Why is all this built of twigs?"

"Look over there, and the corners." Shajee pointed to a stake in the ground and a coil of rope tied to it, the other end fixed to the building.

"See that, kid? These buildings all float."

"They float? Why?"

"The river comes up sometimes, every few years. And they ride it out."

"So this... this is really part of the river itself?"

"Two rivers, actually. The one we been following is joined up. That's why this is the end."

Popey stared at the moorings and thought about all this. Moments ago, people were talking about him becoming a leader, yet now he felt like he knew nothing. Why did this happen? Because he was rich, he realized. Or so they said, he was rich. He didn't feel a bit different, and as he stared at the stake in the ground he realized he wasn't going to act any different. He wasn't stuck into the ground, not yet. There was no rope on his ankle, waiting for the spring flood. He still had his plan to live among the Giants and learn about them.

"Kid, you coming with?" Shajee's words cut the trance like a knife.

"Yeah, Shajee, I'm coming. Where are we going?"

"What if I said you'll see?" Another broad grin.

"Actually, I'd like to know." Popey suddenly felt in charge.

"Huh? OK, there's some outfitters I'd like you to meet, think about getting some new clothes for tonight."

"Allright. Elada after them… in the afternoon, right?"
"Yup, that's it. This way."

The walked down the street, Popey following his usual half step behind. Shajee held himself up a bit higher, perhaps because he was without his pack, and greeted many people passing by. And there were so many, thick and fast, always moving. Popey never saw this much activity in Riverflats. Soon, they came upon a larger stick building with the sign in bright blue letters, "Eddo and Julana, Outfitters". Shajee went to the door, opened it, and stood there for Popey to go in first.

The shop was filled with a rainbow of color, hanging at all angles in the form of clothes. Every size, every style, everything you could imagine. Off to one side were more practical items like packs and small stoves that showed this to be a Traveler's paradise. Popey knew at once why Shajee took him to this store – it would be very familiar to him.

Popey stood there a while, trying to make sense of it, when an older man came out and greeted Shajee as he came in.

"Shajee! I see you have returned! Have a good travel?"
"Eddo! Yes, a great one, in fact! We're here to bring ourselves up a notch, so to speak. Oh, this is Popey, I met him on the way."
The old man finally acknowledged Popey over his glasses. His hair was thin and white, but he had a quick smile and a sparkle in his eyes. "Popey, it is? Nice to meet you."
"It's nice to meet you, too."
"You both had some good luck out there, then?" Eddo spoke to the space between them this time.
"Let's just say that Elada is still working on how good!" Shajee bubbled enthusiastically.
"Well, then," Eddo replied, "Perhaps I should get my daughter to wait on you, young man, while I attend to Shajee. Julana!"

At that call, a young woman came from the back. She was short and stout, but rather attractive. Her dark hair was pulled back in a rather serious way, and it highlighted her dark eyes, which tended to follow her feet. "Yes, father?" she called as she came in, and seeing Popey in front of her knew what her job was. She came over to him quietly and carefully, and Popey felt uncomfortable for her.

Eddo cleared his throat. "I think this young man may want to improve his appearance." Shajee grinned again, "We do have a big party tonight!" "I'd be happy to help. Come with me." Julana said carefully, talking to the floor. And Popey followed her off to the side where some rather bright and happy clothes hung. She continued, "This will bring out the sparkle in your eyes."

Popey bent down a little bit, and suddenly had a wave of boldness come over him. "Tell me about the paths beyond Piketown. Is there anywhere else to go after this?" Julana was stunned by the question, but held her head up firmly. "No, this is it. It's all Giants from here, not really a path. Except for... well, it's a cave I've been to, but no one really lives there now. Too dangerous." Popey was interested in this story. "Tell me more... it's really close in to the Giants? It's where they all live, and no Hopnegs?" Julana smiled, because there was something more going on here than she thought. "That's it. What is it you want?"

Popey fished in his pocket for a while, and pulled out four of the jewels he had left. "Can I get a complete outfit to go there, packs and all, for this?" Julana was amazed. "Yeah, ah, sure, that would cover a lot. But you have to cross the river, and that's very hard!" Popey was happy with this answer, and found himself touching Julana on her arm. "But you've been there! Can you show me how to get across?" Julana gave Popey a long, loving look. He wasn't a poser out to look important, he had his mind on adventure or... something much deeper. "I would be happy to help you, Popey is it? Popey. We can go tomorrow and I'll get you across. With everything you need to live for a year over there, OK?"

This was what Popey hoped for. Shajee had reached the end of his line, and now it was time to go on alone. He could do it, and this young woman was going to show him how. He couldn't stop smiling at the thought. "Thanks," came easily from him, and then a little harder, "You take these. I'll be back in the morning and you get me what you think I'll need. Then we'll go. Do you think you'll need more, this'll do it?" Julana couldn't stop smiling in this moment. "No, this is good, Popey. I'll have you ready to go. Head to the left of the dawn and I'll be ready." Popey finally let her arm go. "OK, thanks. You're great."

Since Shajee was taking his time, Popey decided to waste some on his own looking over all the clothes. They were nice, but he would make do with what he had for now. Julana knew he was just looking, and she liked passing a late morning with him. Finally, Shajee bounded out of the changing room in a beautiful long cobalt coat with a purple shirt and black pants, saying, "I'll take it!" He slammed the jewel down on the counter, got a few coins in change, and Popey turned to him.

"Looks great! Your new outfit?"
"Yeah, I love it! I have to get some jewels sewn into it. You didn't get anything?" Shajee suddenly looked worried.
"Nah, I didn't... see anything I liked." Julana giggled a bit, and waved herself to the back of the store again mouthing, "Bye!"
"Kid, you're not... well, if that's you, it's you. Let's go."

With that, they were out of the store and back over to Elada's shop. When they arrived, Elada kissed Shajee on the cheek again, and pulled his lapels in admiration. "Aren't you the cute one!"
"Ah, cut it out! So what've you got for me, my lovely?"
"Oh, you'll like this!" and she led them to the shop again through the open door.

Two decent sized piles of jewels stood there, the same colors as the bits they collected. "For you, Popey, here are eleven more, not as big and beautiful as before, but good ones. And you, Shajee, have all of these." Shajee whistled. "I'll take it. You, Popey?" Popey didn't need to be elbowed this time. "I'll take it, thank you." It was more than he thought, altogether, and he still had three left from the night before. Perhaps he was rich. No matter.

Shajee had other things on his mind, though. "You going to be at Mitterer's tonight? I think he's got a lot of plans." Elada smiled, "I wouldn't miss it for anything, dear. But I should start getting ready soon. You boys will be OK with all this? Thank you for your business. And Popey..." "Yes, Elada?" Popey wasn't sure what was up. "Popey, you had a chance to talk to Councilor Mitterer, didn't you?"

Popey now knew what was going on. "Yes, I did. Thank you, I'm not sure I'm interested." Elada sighed gently, but was willing to wait until the party to work on him. "I'll talk to you more about it later, Popey. I can see you're a serious young man, and I like that about you. Well, I have some work to do before I get ready. See you both later!"

They said goodbye, and with another kiss on the cheek Shajee slipped out of the door, this time a full step behind Popey.

They went back to their rooms, and Popey spent the afternoon staring at the jewels he had. They were so beautiful, and so much more than he ever thought he would have. All the backbreaking work he had done, raising and gathering seeds, and here one quick adventure brought him so much more. Was he just lucky? Was this all there was to life?

He knew he had somehow found a shortcut, but was determined not to spend too much time on it. After all, Shajee had been traveling much longer, and learned the ways of the Travelers much more deeply. Only now had he found his way into such wealth.

He lay there, half asleep on his bed. It was such a comfortable bed. And in this state of mind he felt the wind inside of him, carrying him on. He felt the earth at his feet, and all over him, and also deep within of him. And the fire in his mind almost made the jewels sparkle all the more. That was it, he figured. It was what was in him that made them so pretty. It was what was in him that made him want to follow the water once more. He'd go to this party, meet a few people, and then be himself again.

With a deep smile, he rolled over and took a nap for the rest of the afternoon. The life of the rich was good, but he still had other plans.

He woke to a sharp knocking on his door. "Kid, you allright?" "Come in, Shajee!" Popey wasn't sure what was up, but he was ready for anything now that he knew what he was doing. "So they're all set up for dinner and all that, let's get at it." Shajee rubbed his hands together, excited at the prospect of a really good, hot meal.

Popey rolled out of bed, combed his hair quickly, and came back to the door. "I'm ready, let's go." Shajee looked at him with disapproval, but his rolling shoulders figured that the serious kid had his own ways. It was then that Popey noticed Shajee had a perfume on, a thick smell of flowers that hung in the air long behind him.

They marched through the hallway again, and out into the most light and festive hall Popey had ever seen. Decorations made of what seemed like jewels hung from everything that stuck up. The dozens or hundreds of lamps were all lit brightly and happily, dancing to... was that music he heard? The band started just as they rounded the corner, as if on queue (and Popey hoped it was not to signal his arrival). Elada, wearing a long bright dress of what looked like pure gold, had her hair up in a tight and elegant knot. She greeted Shajee by just taking his hand this time, and he bowed to her. They were obviously having a lot of fun.

Popey didn't know what to make of it all, and stood there for a while drinking it all in. Eventually, Elada pulled him over and said, "I want you to meet some people. I think you'll like them." "Sure," Popey replied, happy to not feel so out of place now that he'd noticed he was the worst dressed person here, "I'd like that."

They went over to a couple that were middle aged, and Elada pulled the thin-haired man in the black suit aside. "Councilor Desmi?" She cooed softly. "Yes, Councilor Elada?" "I'd like you to meet a very bright young man who has made his own way in the world very well. His name is Popey, and he came from Riverflats."

Popey felt he understood just about everything now. All this time, Shajee was hoping to get to where he was tonight. There he was, handsome and smiling and so sure of himself. He made it. And in turn, he wanted to do Popey a favor, and Popey appreciated it. But it wasn't him, not now at least.

"I'm sorry, young man? I am Councilor Desmi"
"Oh, sorry. I'm Popey. Very pleased to meet you."

The rest of the evening was a blur. Popey ate and talked and even tried to dance once with a very cute girl a bit younger than he was.

But after a while, he had to excuse himself early and head off to bed. After all, he had big plans.

On his way out, he found Shajee. He wasn't sure what to say.
"Thanks for everything, Shajee. I'm heading out tomorrow on my own. I'm glad it all worked out for you, and... I'll catch up with you later."
"Wait, kid, you're sure?"
"Yeah, I am. But thanks. You're a pal."
"Well... you keep your eyes open, kid, OK?"
"Eyes open, Shajee. Eyes open."

And with that, he said goodbye and goodnight.

CHAPTER 15:
BEING DIFFERENT

When Popey woke up, it was still dark. The first purple glimmer of dawn came through the window with the chirp of a cardinal. It was hard to see anything, but a few rubs of his eyes allowed Popey to find his coat. He went to look at the bathtub, but instead found himself saying to it, "Time to get dirty again". With an unseen twirl his coat was on, and he was out the door.

The hallway was much darker, and Popey had to feel his way through it. It made him nervous as he thought of his decision to pass up an opportunity made for him, so heartfelt in gratitude. As he made his way to the end, he thought about the small difference between light and dark, between yes and no. It always seems so important in the moment, but once a decision was made there was nothing to do but see it through. And here he was, wandering in the dark going by nothing but his instinct. He had to keep going.

At the end, the large hall where the party was the night before was still lit by a few lamps. Popey could see some garbage and glasses around testifying to the great time had by everyone. Why wasn't he so cheerful? Why were they the ones who had all the fun? The party must have gone very late, he saw. Shajee was still asleep, no doubt. It must be a great life. Popey was still determined to find his own way, and live with the Giants. He would learn their magic, he would learn their power. But if only he could have found himself comfortable at the party... if only he felt as sure about his life as the people he was leaving behind.

A solid click through the front door, and he was out into the cool morning air. As he turned toward the dawn, now gently orange and red, the whistles of sparrows guided him on. They knew the way as well. He felt it all inside of him now. It was what he had to do, and once again he felt almost as cheerful as the birds about it. He walked down the street with a gentle bounce.

Soon, he had walked his way to the edge of town. The streets were so empty at this time of day, and there was no one there to help him. Popey had hoped that the town would stop on this edge as quickly as it started on the other, but it seemed to slowly fall apart instead. The houses were not as well built, and the roofs pitched at strange angles. This was the poor section, he figured, and he was almost glad to know that not everyone in Piketown was rich. Popey thought of the burdens this town would have, and knew he wasn't ready to take them on for his own. His pace picked up through this part of town, not out of fear but out of a great happiness that he was making the right choice. Soon, however, even this part of town stopped and only grasses were ahead.

Turning to the left of the dawn, he found he was moving faster again. It was a time for action, and he told Julana he would be there at dawn. Still, with all of his walking, the cold air nipped at his ears and pulled his arms in tight over his coat. If nothing else, he was hungry.

That's how the doubts crept up on him again. He knew he was going to have the right equipment to go further this time, but here he was hungry and alone. He still felt he had to live with the Giants, and learn their ways. But who was he kidding? He knew nothing. He had no idea what he was doing. He hadn't even found breakfast yet! It was all so silly. Everyone else seemed to know just what they were doing, and here he was wandering again, without a clue.

But he stomped on, working the cold away. There wasn't much else he could do. This was something that Popey was going to see through, no matter what. A different kind of determination raced in his blood, one that was quieter and less angry than before. He smiled softly as he felt it rise, whatever it was, that would see this journey to the end.

Within a short while, before the sun was more than a glint to his right, he saw the river in front of him. There, just over a bit, was a figure standing, and then waving. It must be Julana. He went into a careful run, and soon was in front of her.

"Hello, Popey!" She greeted him. She had been up for a long time getting this all together. "I was able to do this without anyone knowing. It seemed like a secret, so I thought I should keep it." Popey caught his breath quickly.

"Thanks, Julana. That was nice of you, but I dunno that it's a secret. Well, it was best in the end."
"I knew from my father that they had… other plans for you."
"I know. This is what I want to do."
"What are you doing? Why do you want to go to the land of the Giants?"

Popey fumbled a bit. He didn't like having to explain himself, even to someone so helpful and nice, and pretty as well. "I… I lost everything I had to them, and my whole town just ran away. It was… it seemed like such a stupid thing to do. I want to know about the Giants and their magic and…" He trailed off a minute, not sure he still believed the last part, "I hope that we can some day fight them and not have to run."

Julana looked him in the eyes for a while. She was right about him – he was the adventurous type. It was just a lot more of an adventure than she thought. Slowly, her eyes fell to her feet.

"I was thinking about… maybe coming along with you. Get away from all the… the stuff I have to do. But… well, I don't know if that's something I'm up for."
"Julana, I… I appreciate what you've done, it's just that… I think I need to be alone."
Julana kept staring at the ground. "I understand, I think. I may just get away on my own. The way you… the way you turned them down was really cool, Popey." Her eyes lifted back to meet his. "Not many Hopnegs could do that!"

Popey smiled at this, and looked away in a moment. He saw a huge and very full pack, and a boat with 2 pairs of large oars. He realized then and there that there was business to go over, as the sun was starting to shine full on the river, sparkling and churning.

"Thanks. So what did you get me here?"
"Oh, it's everything. A large pot and a firestick are in the big section, along with lampoil and some canned food. Enough for months, if you can find some seeds on the way. On the side is a saw, a big knife, and over there a lamp. You'll need the lamp for Fountain Cave, when you find it."

Popey was digging through it. It looked like enough for a year, for sure. And all the equipment needed to have a good life on his own. But there were still some questions he needed answered.

"This... Fountain Cave? What is it? Is it the end? How will I find it?"
"It's a cave with good water running through it, and you can't miss it. The trail ends there, nothing but Giants beyond. Many of them live right there as well. If you dare go further, it's up to you to find the way."
"A good place to set up camp, then?"
"Yes, you'll be safe there – all winter if you want."
"And we get over to the other side by boat?"
"Yes, I'll take you over. It's safest this time of day, fewer Giants around."
"OK, then. Thanks a lot Julana, you've helped me a lot." And they both climbed into the boat, Popey's new pack being flung in first.

Julana sat in back, ready to launch. "This is going to be hard, Popey, so paddle for the shore as hard as you can. We'll drift a lot, but don't worry. I'll drag it back along the shore so that I can paddle back on my own, and drift right back here when I'm done. Ready?"
"Ready."

The thought of actually being on the river was as exciting as lightening in his blood, but Popey showed no outward expression at all. Julana untied the boat, and very quickly they started drifting downriver. They both paddled and pulled and strained as hard as they could, not just to move forward but to keep it pointed in the right direction. They made about as much progress across as they did down, and Popey was worried that they were going to lose sight of the shore. Looking over his shoulder a bit, he then saw there was a small point that they would likely crash into one way or the other. That was why this was the crossing point. It was up to the river to pick it for them.

Before long, Popey's arms started to hurt. He wasn't used to rowing. Just as he wasn't sure where his energy was going to come from, they hit the bottom on the sandy beach of the other side. Julana called to him, 'Get out and take the line!" and Popey eagerly raced out to grab the rope and pull it up. Julana scrambled to the front, and soon they were both on shore. They made it, they were in the land of the Giants.

"Whew!" Julana spoke first. "That was good, you're really strong."
"This is it? The land of the Giants?"
"We're here. The trail is..." Julana looked a while. "It's over there, in that clearing. See it?"
"Yes, I see it. Just follow that downriver some more, and it's Fountain Cave?"
"Yes, it may be more than one day, you have a lot to carry now!" Julana blushed when she thought of all the things she lovingly packed away for him. They would be useful one day, but today they would be a burden.

Popey stared at the path, realizing it was very thin and hardly used. He felt adrift, like he was still on the river, instead of standing by it on wobbly legs.

"Last thing, Julana, how will I know Fountain Cave? What do I look for?"
"It's a big cave right at the river. Oh, there's a metal tube put there by the Giants, but ignore that. Go up over that, and you'll see the dry entrance. It's the only small stream that joins the river the whole way."
"Thanks, Julana. You're a great help. Here, I want you to have this... for you, not the store."

Popey fished out of his pocket one of the blue jewels that he thought would look so good with Julana's dark eyes. Julana looked at it a moment, and then at her feet. "Thank you, Popey. You're very kind." She looked back up at him. "I hope you find what you're looking for. I... um, I have to get back now."

"Yeah, I understand. Thanks again. You've been a great help. Bye!"
"Bye, Popey! Good luck!"

Somehow, they managed to avoid hugging each other. Julana turned, and started dragging the line at the front of the boat upriver.

Popey looked back at her for a long time, and then realized that through all of this he still hadn't managed to have breakfast. He saw the great big canteen attached to his pack, and filled it. This water tasted good, but Popey was drawn to the disappearing figure along the beach instead. Then, he turned to see what he had to eat.

A whole bag of his favorite kind of roasted seeds almost called his name as he opened it. He sat there filling himself, as the sun gradually started to warm him on the outside. This would be a long, but good day, he figured. And he was finally completely alone.

He didn't move for quite some time, staring at the river that stood between him and probably every other Hopneg there was. When he finally got up, he tried to move his pack onto his back the way Shajee did, in one quick movement. It was then that he realized just how heavy it was, and how hard it would be to travel today. "Oh well," he said to river, jealous of how effortlessly it slipped along. And he started walking.

Handspan after difficult handspan went past. Between the crushing weight and the need to hunt for the often hidden path, Popey felt like he was making no time at all. The sun had circled him, now falling on his back, but the cool air of the forest he was under kept him from feeling the worst of it. Towards the end of the day, he saw something large and Giant made in front of him – another crossing of stone. This one, however, he knew to go around.

Carefully, he slid his way past, hoping to not be seen. But when he realized it was nothing but fast Demons, again, he stopped worrying. He was invisible. Besides, this was what he wanted, wasn't it? It was the land of the Giants. He was clearly in it. Beyond the stone crossing he stopped, completely exhausted. It was not yet night, but he was done. It was time to rest.

Popey made a shelter as he was shown to, and found that his new saw and knife were excellent tools. When his shelter was done, Popey dug into the pack for whatever else he might have. A small can of meat caught his eye, and then in the bottom – a blanket. This was what was so heavy. He really did have everything. He smiled to himself, and ate his canned dinner more slowly than his hunger wanted to. This would be good, after all.

As the sun dove under the treetops, Popey curled up and slept almost as well as he had on the soft bed the night before.

Chapter 16:
Power of the Heavy

Dawn came quickly, and Popey greeted it with one eye open. A day ago, he was happy to be back on the path, but today he was beaten and sore. He was eager to get moving, but as he sat up he felt just how heavy the memory of his pack was.

Popey stretched himself out, trying to get a sense of what hurt and what he might do about it. But it was no use. All of him was sore, and determined to stay just where it was. Now that he had stopped, Popey would find it hard to be anything but stopped again.

His blanket had kept away the night chill, which was now melting ahead of the sun. The aches were easing, slowly, but this would not be an easy day. He dug in his pack for breakfast, realizing that one way or the other he would eventually feel good enough to get going again. Nibbling on his favorite seeds, it became obvious that trying to ignore the problem, or trying to walk it off, would not work. He would have to sit here, in this moment, and stretch and pull it out.

Once Popey was full, he stood up just outside his shelter. His shoulders, back, and legs all hurt, and hurt bad. He closed his eyes, and stood there – leaning, stretching, turning his neck, rolling his head. "One more day, I think, just one more day," he said to no one at all. Soon, he felt a bit better, and stood there motionless with his eyes closed. A bit of stillness now would make the hike possible, he thought. Gradually, the pinch and hurt drained off of him, and he felt able to get going.

Popey ate a bit more, sitting down and stalling just a while longer. The river in front of him was much bigger than what he remembered – didn't Shajee say it was two rivers joined up? And sure enough, as the sun rose enough to light the whole valley, Popey could see a blue course of water in front of him, and a darker brown like he had seen before on the other side. One river, two parts. They flowed together, but stayed separate. Each rubbed up against the other, but all either seemed to care about was to keep going on, downriver. That's what they did together.

Popey found himself staring at these two rivers in one for what seemed like an whole handspan. It was an entirely different mass of water here. But it was still the same rolling, bubbling run that almost appeared to be standing still until your eye caught it right. It made the whole valley Popey was in, wearing it down over a long time. One part was clear and blue, the other part deep and muddy. Two different sources, two different characters – but they both had one calling.

After a while, Popey felt lazy. He blushed at the thought of the river moving so easily next to his own sore steps that were so hard. There was so much in his heavy pack, and it weighed him down. But he liked having it all, for once. It was good to know he wasn't going to fail just because he wasn't prepared. It was all up to him now, to go downriver. It might not be as easy as it was for the river, but it was something he could do.

On that last thought, he stood up and broke his camp. When the pack thudded down on his back, he winced, but without reason – it didn't hurt after all. The weight held him down just a moment, but then he was off.

It wasn't as hard a day as he expected, once he got used to the idea that he was never going to make fast time. This river seemed unsettled, and twisted and turned more than he was used to. The path happened to follow close to the shore, and rounded alongside every turn in the river with a muddy respect. And there was a lot of mud, in patches, as it wound through the valley.

After a time, the path seemed to end. Up ahead was some kind of crossing where Demons whirred past at amazing speeds. The path went into the sand under this crossing and disappeared. Where did it go? Was the path away from the river, under the crossing like before, or along the river ahead? It was hard to tell, and with all this noise above it was hard to make a decision. Julana didn't tell him about any of this.

Popey felt confused, and sat down. This was a bad day, his first really bad day on the path so far. He knew the decision he had to make couldn't be that hard, but he had a lot of trouble making it.

Traveling, and doing it right, was starting to seem a lot harder than he thought. Still, he figured, it was better than not being ready. That choice was obvious. And then, the choice of which path must be obvious, he figured. It must be along the river, because Fountain Cave was along the river. Of course.

As Popey walked along the sandy beach under the crossing, he felt lonely for the first time. So many things were suddenly so hard, and there was no one to talk to. He shuffled through the sand, thinking about how far it must be. "Can't be too far," he finally blurted out. "It has to be just up here". He felt like a kid again, lost and clueless. A very large Demon plodded along, almost silently, floating like a boat on the river. Eventually, after wandering the beach for a handspan or more, something like a path dribbled out of the woods in front of him. Popey felt slightly embarrassed at having to give himself encouragement, but he also realized that no one else was there to hear how pathetic he sounded.

He kept going just a short while, falling into the rhythm of the path again. Then, up ahead there was something that looked like metal crossing the path. The sun was directly overhead, and the shine from the metal hit him hard. Popey broke into a run, hoping this was the tube he was told about, and staggered under the weight of his pack right into the blinding light. With the roar of Demons overhead, he felt as though he was being attacked on all sides. But that would be what the land of the Giants was all about, wouldn't it?

He stumbled to the metal, and saw that it really was a tube, just as he had been told. Water ran out of it, dribbling into the river and rolling away. He panted a moment, and looked above to see if there was another opening. Seeing nothing, Popey started to climb up the hill. With more of a crawl than a climb, he made very slow progress, lifting all of the weight he had on him. When he stopped after a moment of despair, he felt it. Cold air. It tumbled down the hill from just above, where there must be the entrance to a cave!

To reach the source of the chill, Popey had to pull himself up with his arms. The hillside was too steep for anything else, unless he could get a rope up. For now, however, all he could do was dig his hands in and pull. Up he slid, kicking and struggling the whole way. Finally, he saw a dark hole in the hill, and smelled the cool, damp air coming from it. He had made it to Fountain Cave.

He pulled himself up to the hole, and found he could stand at the entrance. It was much larger than he was. But it was not as big as a standing Giant, so there was some protection. Popey could see why this was a good place to make camp.

Once he caught his breath, Popey carefully stepped inside. It was very dark, and very quiet. Before his eyes could adjust, the only thing that ran across his senses was the sound of water running. Popey knew that he would never be able to see in there, and then realized that he had thoughtfully been given a lamp. He grabbed it from the side of his pack, and then dropped the whole pack to dig out the firestick. After fumbling in the dark a while, he had the lamp lit, and held it in front of him.

What he finally saw he could not believe. This was a large cave, worn into the rock like a river valley. The stream in the middle was clear and bubbly, and as Popey dropped down to get a closer look he smelled and tasted it as good clean water. There were many places to live in here, some already taken by small birds. There were also many places to store food and supplies, and to wait out the winter. And just ahead, above the stream, was an excellent place to keep a fire lit, and keep the cave warm.

Popey knew he would have to explore at least as much of Fountain Cave as he could reach, just to know who or what lived here. As he went off to do this, away from the sun where he could count the handspans, days passed quickly, almost without being noticed.

He found other entrances to the cave, but none were as large as the main one he came in through. Birds flew in and out, mice came and went, all seeking safety just like Popey. The sandstone walls had been carved in all kinds of ways, by animals and water and maybe just falling apart. This was more than just a cave, it was a kind of palace. He wandered through as much of it as he could, mapping it out in his mind by the light of his lantern. It was just as huge as the Giant world, but deep and friendly and homey.

Popey set up a camp just by the large entrance, on a ledge above the tasty water. He even built a small door that swung on a hollowed out stick, just to help keep winter out one day soon. Lastly, he made a firepit where he knew the mysterious winds of the cave would take the smoke up and away.

His new house was solid and quiet, and after many days he knew it was set up just the way he wanted. There was always some more work to make sure it was homey, but Popey felt he was ready to go off and discover the Giants' world firsthand. One morning, he looked over his humble house, lit brightly by a fire and a lamp, and decided it was time to set off and explore. His pack and all his gear would stay behind, safe and secure.

The fresh air was hot, and the sunlight burning as Popey stepped out. He had become used to a world lit by his own fires and vented with its own breezes, deep in the earth. The garish heat of the outside caught him off guard, and he paused a moment. He still felt like a kid, who knew nothing at all, but having the cave secured gave him confidence in himself despite the blast of stepping out into the strange world. Popey promised himself that he would remember this feeling.

What was most strange about the outside of Fountain Cave was the constant roar and whoosh of the Demons above him. Inside, it was silent except for the water, but out here it was nothing but Demons. There had to be more Giants around, and Popey was off to find them. But that constant noise, from the top of the hill, just followed him everywhere. He always remembered to be careful, since he was still just three and a quarter inches tall and deep into the land of the Giants.

There were only two ways to go, and since he had come from one way, Popey decided to continue downriver a short way to see what more there might be. There wasn't a path or any obvious place to follow, so he stayed by the sandy beach of the river. It wasn't exactly safe to be out in this bright light, since it was easy to be seen. He walked on carefully.

After a very short time, he rounded a bend and saw more of the large Demon boats in the river. He stopped, and looked carefully, but the Demons seemed to be asleep. He remembered the last time he was this close, and his heart pounded at the thought. Demons can wake up at any time. When Popey peered around a small rock to take a closer look, he couldn't help but notice that he was once again half in sun, half in shadow. He smiled at it this time, and knew that he had to stick to the shadow. The light was inside of him, after all, and he could go in for a closer look.

Creeping up through some brush and grasses, it became clear to Popey that this was another one of those grain terminals, where the grain is scattered everywhere. There were no Giants around to see him, so he quickly moved around to gather what he could, stuffing his pockets full. Stay to the dark, know the light. It was an easy job to do.

Over the next few days, Popey gathered a lot of these seeds and brought them back to Fountain Cave. They became his main source of food, stretching out what he brought into something that would easily make a whole winter. These seeds were simply everywhere, thrown out unwanted all over the ground. It was a great thing if you were small and needed the food, but it still seemed strange to Popey that so much could be just cast along the beach.

After many trips like this, and no signs of movement at all, Popey became comfortable enough to simply look around. The seeds appeared to come from over the place where the Demons were constantly running and howling. There was a large structure of some kind that dropped them down to these things like boats. Eventually, he became brave enough to climb the hill and stare straight out at where all this came from. And there, across the Demons, were actual Giants. They were standing, not doing much at all, but they were clearly Giants. More importantly, a quick look at the building that went over to them showed that one of the other openings of the cave must be very close by!

Popey ran back to the entrance he used most, slipped in, and shut the door. It was hard to get used to the darkness, so he stood there a moment with his heart pounding. The cave ran over to Giant territory! It was a short-cut to get everything he wanted after all. By the time his eyes became used to the darkness, he was calm again. He went over, snatched his lantern, and started walking.

This turn, then that, over and around. Eventually, he made it to where he thought a small opening would be near the Giants, and set his lantern down where the light hit the cave floor.

He slid up carefully, crawling in the tight space. By the time he got to the top, he was dirty and stiff. But as he poked his head out, he could see that he was right – except that the Giants had moved on in the time it took him to get there. Still, the point was made that he could get around this way. Popey pulled himself all the way out, and looked around. The Demons were speeding and rumbling on the other side of him. He was definitely right. One side of the cave went to the Giants, one went to the river. From here, he could explore everything.

It was starting to get dark outside, so Popey felt brave enough to see a bit more. Some of the smaller structures off to one side looked like they might be Giant houses. Those were interesting to see, since he had never been close to Giants at rest before. It was a long walk, but eventually he made it over to the quiet and orderly houses.

Nothing was happening, and there was nothing to see. But Popey couldn't help sitting in the cool grasses for a long time, watching the sun fall and waiting for something interesting to pop up. It never did. Soon, it was dark, and a few lights came on inside the houses. There was little to see here.

Popey decided to go to work at night, since he would not be seen in the dark and quiet. He went back to his gear, and grabbed a small shovel that he knew would come in handy some day. Going back to the Giant-side opening, he made it wide enough to allow him to walk up without scurrying like a deermouse.

Walking away from his work, he picked up his lantern and followed the way to his camp. He was so comfortable now in Fountain Cave that he almost could have done it without the light. But he was careful, and felt that he was completing something very important. Soon, he could do the work he set out to do.

He sat down by his bed area, and took off his coat. It was filthy, and so was he. Though the stream was cold, it was clean. It was time for another bath, he thought, even though he wasn't sure what it might feel like.

The icy water stung him at first, but gradually he became used to it enough to wade into the stream. He sat there for a long time, soaking in the water, getting clean. Despite the cold, he felt the fire inside of him keeping him warm, and keeping his thoughts fixed on what he would do next.

Popey realized that he could move as he pleased, and go just about anywhere he wanted around here. But the stream always went downhill, down into the river. For a brief moment, Popey thought of doing the same thing. He wanted to follow along downriver some more, curious as to why everyone said not to. But there was a lot to see here – that was obvious.

Slowly the cold and bubbling water sank deep into his thoughts. There was no sound in the cave except the water. It was what the cave was about. And as Popey drifted off to sleep in the pool, his old dream came back to him again. But it was different. This time, he was the wood duck whistling off in the distance, first dabbling through the mud and then taking off into the dawn on the breeze that ruffled the cordgrass.

As he woke up from this dream, he was cold and wet, but smiled the easy way he only could when at home. Fountain Cave was his home. And Popey thought it was about to unlock many secrets.

CHAPTER 17:
UNLEARNING

As the days went by, the air outside slowly became cooler. The longer nights gave Popey more time to be out under the cover of darkness. Both of these made it possible for him to go further away from the side entrances of Fountain Cave without carrying even a canteen for refreshment.

Night exploring, however, was not very useful. The Giants were often around during the day, but when the sunlight dimmed into a lavender twilight they usually had already left. Whatever went on here, it happened during the day. This seemed odd to Popey, since there were so many bright lanterns all over. But whatever the reason for them, it wasn't to do more work.

The area he came up under was a strange one, with many odd things around. The largest was another mountain made of round, tall buildings, just like he saw before. This must be where that grain was stored, just as the other place. There was much more, however, to this mountain. For one, there were long metal ribbons set into the ground, with wood apparently holding them together. Each was as tall as Popey, and shiny enough to be slippery on the top.

Popey studied these long and hard, hoping to find out why they were there. He had earlier seen a large Demon-like thing sitting on them, but was too scared to go out and look. Now, in the failing light, there was little to be worried about – but not much to learn, either. The whole place was dead, with no life at all. There was nothing more than those incredible lanterns, which kept it bright all night.

Back upriver a bit, the Giant houses also held no clues at all. They were incredibly still, as if Giants had no interest in being outside. Every once in a while, a Demon of some kind would arrive, and Giants would leave it behind for the house. But this happened so randomly, Popey never could make any sense of it. After days and days of watching, he felt no closer to his goal.

Since he slept in a cave, Popey found himself sleeping during the day and exploring at night. Even though he felt like he was making little progress, it felt great to have time alone, just being in the Giants' space. He thought about all the things he had been told about Giants from the time he was a kid. Stories about how vicious they were, hunting down and killing any Hopnegs they saw, kept him alert and hidden. And there were the stories about the incredible magic they had, a magic that came from what they owned. They could harness this power to, with a simple turn of their wrist, change the earth itself into something very different – something cold and hard.

Popey saw evidence of this power around him, with the gray and cold and hard patches all over. But he never saw any of the Giants make them this way. It was just dead and lifeless all night long. The thick air that settled low in the night gave it the feeling of being a graveyard.

It would someday be time to go out during the day, Popey realized, and once he knew his way around he had confidence in being able to do it. But a strange feeling kept coming back to him about the Giants. It was as if everything he had been taught was somehow wrong. Perhaps there was more to this than he thought? If that was the case, extra care would have to be taken during the day. It meant that he had no idea what he was up against, if nothing else. It also meant that he still had to keep his eyes open, and open wide.

Popey went to sleep one night, rather than stay up, just to get his schedule back with the sun. It was hard to go to sleep, knowing that tomorrow was going to bring an exploration in bright daylight. Besides, he was starting to have doubts again – not about himself, but about everything he thought he knew. He came here to learn about the Giants, but it seemed that instead he was unlearning what he thought he knew. Whatever. It would all be clear in the morning – or at least it would be as clear as his bravery would take him.

The morning came hard for Popey, since he was on a different time for so long. The fire by his bed was just a thin smoldering pile, and the lamp was off. It was always hard to wake up in this darkness, but especially so when you aren't used to the time of day.

All the while he stirred the fire and ate and got dressed, Popey had no idea where the sun would be. When he went to his door to check, he could see that it was just past dawn a little bit. He made it, right when he wanted to be up. It was time to explore and see something new.

By now, he could go through Fountain Cave without his lantern lit at all. His world was so close and safe here, and he knew it perfectly. Nothing got past him anymore. He made his way to the bigger back entrance he had carved some time before, and poked his head out. It seemed quiet. He pulled his whole body out, crouched down, and looked. There were a few Giants, over there, by the metal ribbons!

Popey crept slowly over, wondering how he would be able to get close enough to find out what was going on. He was so excited, he didn't even notice at first that what the Giants were gathered around was one of the Demons, or really a long set of them. The Demons were two or three times the size of the Giants, and sat there asleep. The Giants were mostly just standing there, except for a few up close to the end Demon. They appeared to be working on something, and stirred up a cloud of dust and sweat and language.

After watching them for a long time, Popey realized that most of them were not moving or doing much. It seemed safe to move over, if slowly, and get a better look. He wanted more than anything to learn what they were doing, just standing by the Demon. It seemed like so little was going on, but perhaps this was one of their secrets.

He crept over, one hand at a time, staying under the grasses. Sweat poured down into his eyes as the hot sun shone full on his back. Between the glare and the sting, it was hard to see anything. But Popey pressed on, sure that his longtime goal was in sight.

It felt like an entire handspan before he made it over. Push with the feet, pull with the hands. One after the other, he gradually made his way. The excitement of what he would discover ran hot in his blood, and made his heart race. By the time he reached the group, the sun was beating down on him hard, and his green coat stuck with sweat to his tired body. The Giants hardly moved the whole time. There were three of them, standing there, apparently just talking. Popey felt that luck was with him as he stopped, within earshot, to listen.

"I dunno what to do here"
"What do you mean?"
"She says she's taking the kids to Brainerd."
"You can't let that happen!"
"Does she have family there or something?"
"You have rights, too, you know. Fight her!"
"But I can't stop her from moving."
"You need custody, that's the key. Make sure you get it."
"I just don't know where it all went wrong."
"You can't think about that. You have to fight now!"
"You have to fight for your rights."
"I don't want to fight, I... I just want it to be over."
"Don't you give her anything you'll regret later!"
"Yeah, if you just want to get it over, you'll do something stupid, and regret it forever."
"I just have no control over any of this."
"That's why you need a lawyer!"
"We agreed no lawyers, we don't want this to get ugly."
"What? You need to... I know a guy, he's a good lawyer."
"Don't let her screw you over, man!"
"I don't want this to be a fight."
"She's taking the kids away to Brainerd!"

Popey listened and listened to this. When he crouched down in the grass, he expected to be let in on a great secret. He thought that a short while with the Giants, and he would learn all about them. But here they were, arguing like Hopnegs. One of them seemed upset, and the others were trying to encourage him. Popey had seen this scene before. And as it became clear that the words themselves were not important, he stared at the Giant in the middle who seemed upset. Popey studied this Giant's face, which was sleepless and beaten. He wasn't a powerful Giant at all.

The more Popey sat there, the more pitiful all of them appeared. They seemed to be in a bad situation, and they were trying to pull answers out of the air with language. The way they went on, it was clear that no answers of any value were being found. They were desperate, and their hunched over bodies with occasional outbursts of hand waving anger showed it, without hearing any of the words they used.

It was fascinating, but not worth being seen, Popey figured. He turned around and started the slow crawl back to where he came from. This time, he was cool and peaceful. But somehow, it was harder to go back to Fountain Cave. The way over promised so much more than he saw. All he got for his effort was a pathetic group of Giants, no more powerful than he was. It was as if all the stories he had heard were wrong. They must be wrong, Popey finally figured, because these are not killers. They have as much control over their lives as he has over his, if not less.

Over the next few days, Popey wandered over to the Giants a few times, but never heard anything more important. It was usually just small talk, like any of his friends. Most of the time, Popey found it useful to just stand back and watch what they did from a distance.

When a group of Demons pulled into the large yard, all the Giants would scatter. After the Demons stopped to rest, the Giants would come out and do things around them. It went on this way for days, and it was never obvious what was going on. Were they working on it? Repairing it? Popey was never sure. It was the same thing, day after day. The days kept getting shorter, and the air cooler. More and more of the Demons came in every day, in a constant whine of motion and noise.

All of this odd behavior puzzled Popey no end. He came here to figure out the Giants, and their strength. Mostly, what he saw was them standing or sitting around, waiting for Demons to come by.

Watching the houses that were off to the side was no better. The faster and smaller kind of Demons stopped there a lot, but the Giants acted the same way. They were either getting in the Demons, or waiting for them, or apparently sticking their hands deep inside for some reason – to fix them? It was all so confusing.

For years, Popey was taught that Demons served the Giants. They always seemed to go together, at least. But as he thought back to the Giants he saw by the Demon that leveled his house, they were doing the very same thing. It was like the Demons were actually in charge, and the Giants were there only to watch them. Could that possibly be true?

As Popey thought about this possibility, he looked out over the Giants in a different way. And it did seem that they spent their lives in service to the Demons, not the other way around. If the Demons were there to serve the Giants, why did the Giants spend so much time working with the Demons? It was obvious, he thought. The Giants, with every action and thought, serve their Demons. And when they are just standing around and talking, they are totally powerless by themselves.

This still didn't make any sense to Popey. After all, it was obvious that the Demons weren't alive in the same sense he and the Giants were. There was something about the way they slept that seemed like a deep magic, that betrayed they were dead. So how could the Giants serve these dead things that appeared to be conjured by them in the first place?

When he realized this, Popey spent a lot of time deep in Fountain Cave thinking. He was tired of watching and listening and trying to make sense of it all. He would simply figure it out on his own, and then see if he was right. One thing was sure to him, though – what he was told about the Giants was definitely wrong, at least where it mattered the most.

Passing the days in the cave, Popey realized how much he had unlearned in such a short time. It was confusing, coming all this way to learn more and feeling that he now knew less. This had to sink in before he could do anything with it. After all, if the Giants were as pathetic as they looked, how did they destroy so much? Was it the Demons he should look to for his answers, even though they were dead?

Slowly, his old prejudices about Giants dropped away. They seemed so clueless, and by themselves so powerless. It wasn't about the Demons, since they were dead on their own, and only the Giants could give them life. Since it couldn't be the Demons, it had to go back to the Giants, somehow. They used the Demons, but they also relied on them. They needed their Demons to live the lives they had. They were a source of power, a source of everything they owned.

Without thinking, Popey pulled out the jewels he had stored away in a corner of the cave. By the dim lantern, they sparkled as if making a light of their own. He had no idea why he went to these jewels, but something was bubbling up in his brain, an echo of the stream that ran through Fountain Cave.

Slowly at first, carefully, it came to Popey. The Demons were a source of power –that's what they were for the Giants. Just like so many Hopnegs who got to be leaders because they could buy their way in, so many Giants had power they were clueless about just because they were rich enough to buy it. Like Rouger flashing his jewels, these Demons were a visible and frightening source of power. They were guarded and tended to just like jewels, and shown off and used for power in the same way, too.

The Giants had become their Demons, just as the Hopnegs had become scurrying little collectors of jewels. Popey rolled his over and over in his hands, staring at them again for more inspiration. But that was all they were to give for now, except for more and more sparkle.

Popey breathed in hard, and let it out slowly. He had just unlearned everything he knew about Hopnegs, as well as Giants. And there, by the lantern light, a Shajee grin slowly spread across his face. So many things were so obvious now. He had unlearned enough that a lot of things made sense to him that never did before. And Popey realized he had no reason to creep around and fuss with the Giants again. He had seen enough to keep him going without doing anything for a long time.

CHAPTER 18:
LOOKING FAR

The days started to pass very slowly for Popey, once he stopped being so obsessed with the Giants. At times, he wondered why he was still living in Fountain Cave and not the comforts of Piketown. But these feelings would pass as he looked around and saw that he had just about everything he needed. He was, however, very lonely.

At times he would go out just to look at what the Giants were up to, hoping to still learn some more about their magic. He found about the same thing every time. There was no magic that was all that different from what a Hopneg had. It seemed more reasonable to Popey to spend time in Fountain Cave thinking about what he had seen and making sense of it.

As weak as the Giants seemed, they still changed the earth around them. There was a puzzle in all of this, something that had to be solved. Popey still thought about how he might use what he had learned to fight the Giants, and not scurry away, even though that idea already seemed like a far off fantasy.

Popey often sat by the stream with his lantern. He would just sit there, listening to the water and imagining it slowly carving out Fountain Cave. He realized from looking above him that the Giants had built their Demon path over the top of where he was. But Fountain Cave was still there, still being built by the water. In his loneliness, he felt that the splashing and swirling waters were the only real friend he had, telling him some story he didn't yet understand.

Days passed as he sat there, going away only to eat and sleep. Even then, he was never far, and the language of the stream slipped him off to sleep every night. It was in his dreams as well. It seemed so much more interesting than the Giants, and so much more powerful in the end.

Gradually, Popey found himself thinking of Piketown more than he wanted to. It would soon be winter, and he had to make the final preparations to see that his home was dry and warm. The idea that a safe town was only two days away was tempting, though. One night, Popey had a dream of Piketown and River Flats, in the same place, where his friends were all together. He was building suffocating traps for the deermice, alongside floating homes with ropes. When he woke up to the familiar song of the stream, he realized this was his first real dream in a while. It clearly meant something.

That day, Popey knew he should spend time preparing for winter. But the fact that he had a new dream brought a smile to his face that reflected off the stream in wavy lantern light. He thought about all the hard work he had done, keeping the deermice out, and all the hard work it must be to float an entire town. By now, his friendship with the stream, and its reflection deep inside of him, led Popey to think that the stream would give him an answer like he used to get from Emily.

Eventually, the stream gave him a startling answer, one that lit the lantern light in his eyes and made it sparkle like jewels through the cave. Hopnegs were like the stream, making their homes as slowly and carefully as they could. Giants were like the stream, carving out their world as well. They were all forces on the earth, all in their own way. The difference was that the stream was never lost, it always found its way downhill. Hopnegs and Giants both can become lost, and fight their way up. There was no barrier between any of them, especially since they shared the same earth. Even the deermice were only trying to survive. The only difference between any of them was how arrogant they were.

Popey left the stream to start doing his work, carefully. There wasn't that much to be done in the end. He had done most of it in little pieces. He smiled the whole day, as he realized how far he had come to understand something he could have understood just by staying home and thinking. That's when he remembered why he left – his home was destroyed. That was the problem, wasn't it? But this was his home, now. He could let that all go. He could spend a lot of time simply thinking and dreaming his way through the problem. He smiled as he though about how little his adventures spying on the Giants told him in comparison.

As he finished securing his door and checking that his grain was safe from voles, Popey realized that he still had no answer as to how to fight the Giants. It seemed hopeless. His heart sank when he thought about his goal and how far away from it he was now. As much as he managed to unlearn, and as much as he was able to dream beyond that, a useful way of defeating the Giants seemed if anything further from his reach.

As the days passed, Popey would still wander out for a bored look, but his heart wasn't in it. He found that since his last great chat with the stream he always had a small smile as he looked out on the Giants. We are all the same, he figured, and they don't even know I am here. But he never learned anything new, and the Giants always looked as clueless as ever.

One day, the winds of the cave changed. Popey was awakened by the smoke from his fire reaching out and grabbing him, as if alarmed that it could not go out its usual way. Popey got up and went to his door, and saw that the strong wind carried on it a binding cold and a few flakes of snow. That was the end of any ideas of heading for Piketown. Travel in the winter was usually deadly for Hopnegs.

The days dragged on after that, since Popey couldn't go out very often at all. When he did manage to shoulder his door open against the snow, there was not a lot to see outside. The world was white and cold and slippery. The Giants appeared to have disappeared. That was one more way they were like Hopnegs – they didn't seem to go out as much in the cold.

The stream slowly dried up, thinning out to a trickle. This worried Popey, since it was not just a friend, but the source of all his drinking water. What was left wasn't as clean and clear as before, but a bit sandy and harsh tasting. Still, it was possible to spend his days listening to what was left of the stream, even though it was more of a whisper. Struggling to hear it only made it more mysterious to Popey, who knew that his best thinking was done beside it.

One day, the wind howled so strongly that Popey had to put out his fire completely. He didn't like doing that, since it would soon get very cold in Fountain Cave. He shivered for a day, feeling the ice creep up from the door along the walls in thin needles. He huddled under his blanket, passing the time shivering quietly. Eventually, the storm passed, and when Popey had his fire re-lit he realized that the stream was back in full strength. It was saltier tasting, but still mostly clean. It took days of roaring fire to get Fountain Cave warm again, but when it was, he could sit by the stream all day again and think.

It was at this time that Popey realized the stream itself changed, just as he changed. He understood all that he had gone through, all because of the Giants. The stream also went through its own cycles and changes, but it didn't seem to care. It came through in the end, as soon as there was more water.

To fight the Giants, he figured, was just as arrogant as the Giants themselves. If they were all part of the same earth, sometimes one would fight with the other. Piketown might flood, or the Giants might send their Demons out over a Hopneg town. Holding onto the town as something that had to be saved was the same as trying to own the earth. The Giants claimed to own the land, but here was a stream rebuilding a cave right through their little plans. They didn't have any special magic – they were just kidding themselves. Everyone was kidding themselves.

As for fighting the Giants, Popey felt that idea wash down the stream and out of Fountain Cave. There were more important things to worry about than River Flats and what happened to it. The arrogance of the Giants still bothered him, and seemed worth fighting. But not just for the land – that idea was as arrogant as the Giants in the first place.

It was still cold in the cave, and this last thought shivered out of Popey. It would be many days before spring, and he would be stuck here the whole time. They passed slowly, with no new thoughts and no new dreams. But Popey had a smile through all of them. Gradually, however, the stream flowed a little more each day. Soon, it was a flood of water that showed that spring was outside the door.

Popey went out one day, and found the snow had melted. It was muddy and sticky, but he did not have to tramp through it to see that the hill of Fountain Cave was green and alive. Many days would pass before he would do more than just sun himself by the door. That was quite a lot, though, and it made him feel very warm.

One day, Popey was inside sitting by the stream when he heard something outside. Was it another vole? A bird? The strange shuffling turned into a hard knock, and then a call.

"Popey? Are you in there?"

Popey had no idea what was going on. But when the panic drained back out of him, he recognized the voice. It was Lilly! She had come all this way to see him! He ran to the door and wrenched it open, nearly pulling out his carefully made hinge. And there, in front of him, were Lilly and Emily both.

"Popey! You're here!" cried Emily.
"Em, Lilly, I... can't... believe it!" Popey stuttered back.

Popey hugged Emily first, and then Lilly. He felt Emily shiver, and realized she was wet and muddy. He turned to invite her in, but realized that he did not bring his lantern – and these Travelers would not know their way around in the dark like he did. He excused himself, "Back soon," and ran to get it. Popey then led the way to his humble, but dry and warm home.

"This is where I live, come in, you'll love it. Are you hungry? I have porridge!"
"Thanks, Popey," Emily blushed, "I could use something warm."
"And you Lilly? Wow, it's great to see you!" Popey was jumpy with excitement as he scooped out the meal.
"Yes, Popey," Lilly added, "I'd love some."
"How did you two find me here?"
Lilly spoke first, "We came to find you, and wintered in Piketown. Misha came with us that far."
Emily continued, "And everyone in Piketown was talking about you, Popey. You're very well known!"

Popey realized Emily was blushing, and blushed right back at her. "I… well, I… thanks. Were you worried about me?"
Lilly started to snap, but pulled herself back. "I always… I worried about you a lot, Popey, but I can see you've done well here."
Emily had other thoughts than danger. "Did you learn what you wanted to? Can we fight the Giants?"

Popey folded his hands under his chin, and took a long time to think about what he was going to say. "I learned a lot, and it will take time to tell you all of it, but I have no ideas on how to fight, or even if we should."

Lilly looked disappointed as she set her cup down, but Emily downed what was left in hers and reached into her pack. "I have a lot to tell you, too, Popey. I have been Misha's student. This is The Book, and I can read it. I'd like to tell you what I learned, too." She easily pulled out a large, skin covered slab and placed it on her lap as it if was no big deal.

Popey had no idea what to say. He had learned to almost hate The Book and how everyone thought it said everything about everything. But to finally see it in front of him, especially after all he learned, brought out a sense of awe. If Em was a student, maybe she learned something he hadn't. He remembered what Misha told him about the old weak magic that was a part of nature – if anything, Popey learned, the magic of nature was quite strong in its own time.

They sat on some rocks and talked for many handspans, bringing Popey up to date on the gossip about everyone he left behind. Rouger started a new town, further out, and most of River Flats followed him. It was called Prairie Meadows. Rodele simply disappeared after the big fight, and was never heard from again. Lilly and Em convinced Misha that she was too old and frail to rebuild with the others, and they escorted her to the safety of Piketown.

Popey was able to join in with his stories of the same things he saw on the way. He was saddened to hear that Misha had to be carried part of the way, and wished he had been there to help. He felt quite guilty about this, but Emily made it sound as if it was not that difficult.

Misha repaid the favor by making Emily her student, as she had promised Popey. Emily had long stories about spending the winter learning to read The Book and other things. Lilly had enough jewels from selling what she had to put them all up in Mitterer's Hotel for the whole winter.

The whole time they were bringing each other up to date, The Book sat in Emily's lap. It would bounce up and down when her leg got jumpy, and the large skin cover kept catching Popey's eyes. He was dying to know what was in it. But the thought that Emily wanted to talk about all the other Hopnegs first, before digging into The Book, made Popey's now permanent smile even bigger. She still had her priorities right. He was glad she was here.

The conversation stopped after Popey told about being offered a job as a Page. Lilly had heard this in Piketown, and she wasn't sure what was wrong with her brother to reject such a good job. Emily was clearly very proud of him for sticking to his dream, however. An unspoken argument hung in the lantern-lit air, and curled over with the smoke from the now dying fire. Popey felt the tension between the two, and knew he was in the middle of it. His smile faded slightly. Emily was, understandably, the one who knew how to get out of the situation. She leaned over to Popey, her body hiding The Book completely, and told him, "Popey, you really look happy here. Tell me, what have you learned?"

Popey smiled again, and softly told her, "Em, I've learned a lot about the Giants, by watching them. But I have to tell you that for all I learned in my travels, I learned the most just being here, listening to this stream."

Lilly was now sure her brother was nuts. "Popey, what do you mean?"

Popey turned to her and said, quietly, "I learned that the real answers are inside us, and really obvious if you just listen. But the way that we all know isn't the real way, and even when we name it we don't call it by its real name."

Emily's eyes glowed like the lantern. "That's almost exactly what Misha told me, Popey."

CHAPTER 19:
SKILL

Popey and Emily stared at each other a moment, not saying a thing. Swimming through their minds was the idea that they had been through a similar experience that brought them together, even though they had been apart for so long. Neither of them knew what to say. Lilly sensed what was going on, and carefully stood to walk away. In the silence, Popey absent-mindedly scratched his arm, slowly pulling his sleeve up.

"Popey, what's that on your arm?" Emily was glad for a new topic, but alarmed by what she saw.
"Wha? Oh, that. I dunno, I was cut sometime."
"It looks terrible! Let me bandage it!"
Emily carefully took The Book off her lap, and motioned to set it down. First, however, she dusted the spot carefully to be sure it was smooth.
"No, it's... oh, OK. I have some things over..."
Lilly came back at the sound of trouble and a chance to be of help. "I have it. Here we go, here's the cloth."

In a moment, Popey was wrapped up and not scratching again. He smiled at how his sister and friend could never turn their back on him, coming back here only to take care of him again. But a quick glance over to The Book drew his attention back to where they were before.

"Emily, you have to tell me. What's in The Book?"
"Oh, Popey. A lot of things. I have to show you."
"Can you show me where it says that one Rouger said all the time... 'the clever can win against the fastest runner'?"
Emily reached for the book, but stopped and dropped her head slightly. "Popey, I can't find it. It's not in there."

Popey said nothing, but felt as though a few more things were making obvious sense. It was the absence of any other sense that did it for him. Slowly, he started to nod his head and frown. He spoke slowly and carefully. "Let's start over, then. What does it actually say?" Lilly sat down next to him, apparently unaware of this problem before now as well. She was strangely silent.

Emily sat down with The Book on her lap again. This time it was spine-down, with her hands on the sides as though trying to catch it. Slowly, she let it go, and it split in half. She turned the pages reverently, speaking slowly to her friends.

"It has three parts, called 'History', 'Life', and 'Magic'. I think you will the first part especially interesting, Popey. Are you ready?" The book had slowly opened on her lap.
"Yes, Emily, I'd like to hear it."
Lilly added softly, "So would I."
Emily turned into the lantern light, swallowed hard, and spoke as carefully as she could. "Part One, History."

"I am Grosver, and I am too old to flee with the others. But that is what they do. Our home for countless generations has been here, at Great Oaks. It is on the flat land among the oaks, above the creek that leads to the great river. I tell you all this because I am sure it is all ending. The Giants have drained the creek, and are building their homes all around us. Many of us who refused to leave were simply flattened."

The lantern light flickered like a tickle around Emily's soft face as she bent her head down. She paused only long enough for Popey's heart to flutter at how she could read.

"All around us, the Giants have chased us away. Not only here at Great Oaks, but also at Fountain Cave and Swamp Bottom, the Giants and their Demons have come to chase us."

Popey looked up. "Fountain Cave?"
Emily smiled back, "Yes, Popey, you are the first Hopneg to live in Fountain Cave in a long time. Have you found signs that we lived here before?"
"No, Emily, but the Giants have changed this all around, and put that... that Demon path on top."
Emily sighed. "Oh. Oh well."
Popey nodded. "Everything is gone. Even the path they left on is nearly gone."

Lilly looked amused, but a bit annoyed. "Can you keep reading? You know I love it when you tell me this!"

They read on for a long time, but Lilly gradually became restless. She had heard this all before, back in Piketown. Eventually, they all became hungry and had to stop for a long healthy dinner. It was another chance for more gossip and stories, which stretched long into the night.

The next day Popey was proud to make a hot breakfast. It was his way of showing how much he appreciated them all being there. But it was Emily that spoke up first.

"Popey, would you like me to teach you to read as well?"
"Me?"
"Yes, you. I'm sure you can. It's very easy."
"Easy?"
"Yes, Popey. Let me teach you." She smiled almost carelessly, "You can be my student."

Lilly was not excited at this, but had an idea of her own. "Popey, before you do this, can you show me where the Giants are? I'd like to... see what you were talking about for myself."
"Sure, Sis, I can... well, why not?"

So Popey led Lilly along the long winding corridors and showed him his opening. He taught Lilly some of the patterns he saw in their behavior, so that she would be safe. She listened carefully, fidgeting her excitement out of her.

When Popey returned to Emily. She was waiting in the same place. She smiled when he came back, and showed him another book she had – one with letters and pictures. And for many days, they went on the same way. Lilly went to see what Popey had seen before, Popey sat to learn from his one and only favorite teacher, Emily. Popey felt like a kid again, but this time it was a feeling warm with care and nurture. He liked it a lot.

The days passed in quiet routine. Lilly went off to see the Giants, and Popey and Emily stayed back to continue their lessons. One of these days, which seemed like all the others at breakfast, became something else by the afternoon. Lilly ran back from the Giants in a hurry of excitement and noise. She came to the place where they were all living, and stopped short. Popey was holding The Book.

"Lilly!" Emily shouted, "What's up?"
"Ah, I'll tell you… Popey, are you reading The Book?"
Popey nodded his small smile up and down. "Yes, Sis. Do you want to hear? I like this section."
"Popey, I'd love to… you can read it… I'm so proud!"
Popey cleared his throat. "This is from the section called 'Life'." With round lips and a ticking tongue, he carefully rolled the letters out of his mouth.

"In this new world, we have to be true to who we are as Hopnegs. We must be sure that those who are feeling low and broken are raised up. We have to comfort those who have lost someone. Remember that those who are humble and closest to the earth really own it, and those who simply want justice are the ones who get it. Only by showing mercy can you have it shown back to you. If your heart is clean, and you work to make peace, you will be a part of a greater spirit. This may make others accuse you of terrible things and say lies about you, but keep your mind on the greater spirit of the world. We must all be this example of how we can live, despite what happens around us. It is our very life that depends on it."

Popey stopped to see his sister's reaction. In the lantern light, he could see his mother looking back at him with pride lifting her face. He wanted to continue, but found tears in his eyes instead. Besides, he knew Lilly had something to say. But it was Emily who spoke first.

"Lilly, you had something to tell us, about the Giants?"
"Yes," Lilly replied, "I… I heard them talking… about their names, or something like that. I heard the most wonderful names for us!"
Popey was confused. "What do you mean?"
"I mean… that we're in the land of the Giants, right? We should have Giant names! It's like starting over again!"

Emily tilted her head. "I think I should have a new name. I feel like a new person."

Lilly was glad to have Emily going along with her. "I want to be called 'Lilly', and I think you should be called 'Emily'. And you, my brother, you can be 'Joe'."
Emily giggled her reply, "I like 'Emily'! I'd like to be called that!"
From this time on, Emily and Lilly would never tell anyone their old names, no matter what.

Popey didn't look too happy. Emily put her hand on his cheek, carefully. "What about you, 'Joe'?" She giggled again.
Popey blushed, and dropped his head down. "I don't think... I'm just Popey. That's who I am. Besides, I don't think names are all that important after all."
Lilly frowned slightly. "You don't like 'Joe'? I can get you another one."

Popey got up and stretched. "Call me what you want, but I'm Popey. That's it." When he looked over at Lilly, he could see she was disappointed. "It's OK, Sis, it's just that I have a feeling I haven't found a different person here, I found myself. I don't feel so small anymore, but I think that I never did until I let everyone else and those... Giants make me feel small."

Lilly smiled back at him. "I understand. Your name is yours, I wouldn't want to take it."
Emily decided to get between them and let the subject drop easily. "Lilly, did you learn anything out there today?"
"No," Lilly continued, "Nothing more than that. Popey was right, they are a sad bunch. I get the feeling I can teach them more than they can teach me!"
Emily snorted out the laugh of a friend hearing what she expected. "I can only imagine... Lilly. I have to get used to that, Lilly."

Popey started getting dinner ready without asking if anyone else was hungry. He knew they would be, and thought it was just his turn to care for everyone else. He measured out the grain by sight and feel, knowing when it was right. It's the way he did it. The little details of life were suddenly both very unimportant to him, and yet so important because he was hungry. What he did for his sister and his friend were both ordinary, and yet from some place deep inside of him.

After dinner, Popey felt very out of place. He wanted to read more of The Book, but felt strange asking if everyone else wanted to hear it. Finally, after washing and putting the cups away, he got up the courage to prove himself again to his teacher.

"Uh, Emily... that's so new... Emily, I'd like to read The Book again. The part on Magic."
"Popey, that would be great! Why that section?"
"We haven't seen it yet. I'm curious."
"OK, Lilly, you want to hear it?"
"I'd love to! That sounds great!"

Popey got the book out, and sat by the lantern. He opened it near the end, and flipped the pages carefully until he found what he wanted. His voice was more clear, but still careful.

"It is what they own that separates the Giants from us, and is where their magic comes from. We never hold more than we can carry, but they claim to own the earth itself. They have all kinds of things that beat the earth into a different shape, and large animals that they have bent to their will with the harnesses they own. Their magic comes from this. I tell you, you must avoid this corruption. Find yourselves plenty of space so that you cannot see the Giants that live around you. This is the home you should seek. Their magic is not for us, if we are to remain alive and remain ourselves."

Popey stopped for a moment. There was a lot more to this than he thought. Emily saw his look of surprise, and spoke to him softly.

"Popey, I know what you're thinking. But you saw this yourself. You learned it and made it a part of you before you even saw The Book. It shouldn't shock you."
"Emily, it's just that... if all this has been known all along, why aren't we living this way? Why did I have to come here to find it?"
"Popey, you... you didn't really have to. You said so yourself. But it worked for you, and that's what's important. I got the same message by reading it."
"But it's all just junk! Everything we lived with was... oh, I don't know." He was beaten. "We know the truth now."
"Yes, we do. That's what counts. Keep reading?"
"Yeah, allright."

"As I have watched the destruction and senseless murder take place, one thing has become obvious to me – that the Giants never can destroy everything. There is always a family of voles, there are always grasses, there are always more trees. This is our shelter, this is life. As weary as our daily march becomes, through desolate and gray spaces we once knew to be alive, we must remember this. The way of life is always there, and always obvious if we dare to see it."

Popey looked over the book at Emily. She was expecting him to continue, but he had something else on his mind.
"Em, did you get a chance to climb out of the river valley and look at it from the edge?"
"No, Popey, we followed the path to Piketown. Did you?"
"Yeah, I did."
Lilly understood a few things better now. "Is that where you found the jewels?"
"Yes, sis, It was up there, where Giants live and... well, I can't say for sure."
Emily steered him back. "So what were you going to tell us about it, Popey?"
"Well, I didn't appreciate it much at the time, but from up there you can see the whole valley. It's very beautiful, and very... alive, as Grosver says."
Emily felt a bit left out. "You know I'm not good at noticing simple things around me, Popey."
Popey turned his head slightly. "You have The Book, and I have my travels. At least we can both understand each other, Emily. I'm glad for that."
Emily blushed. "I'm glad we have both, Popey."
Popey cleared his throat and went on.

"Never be afraid. There is comfort enough for your wherever you go, if you are comfortable with yourself. This is the most personal kind of magic there is. Do not let yourself be ruled by anyone you do not think deserves the position."

Lilly snorted at this. "If you are comfortable with yourself. That's a lot to ask, sometimes."
Emily looked at her friend. "Yes, but it is important."

"It's so hard to be comfortable with things outside of a… a routine. You both talk about such big ideas, but I've always been… well, unsure about all of that."

Popey stepped in quickly. "I don't think it's about this or that way of doing things, it's about what works best for you to see it all."

Emily dropped her head, and lifted it, to reveal a smile. "Popey, you really have thought a lot here in Fountain Cave! Keep reading, please?"

Popey continued as if nothing had happened.

"The Giants do big things, but not simply because they are big. They also seem to answer to rulers far away. Giants do what they are told and work in groups. What they own makes them think they are individuals, and that is what makes it magic. The people who tell them what to do are royalty or some other far-off people who make the rules. They use noise and nonsense to tell a good story."

Popey stopped again. He knew that Hopnegs never worked well together, and this always bothered him. It made more sense to him to come together, somehow. But if that was the way of the Giants, could he rely on it? He finally had to ask his sister what she thought.

"Lilly, does this sound familiar? We were always trying to organize the crews back at River Flats to work together."

"Yes, you're right. I always wondered why I wasn't a better leader than I was."

Emily hated that talk. "Lilly, I don't think it was all your fault. It's the way Hopnegs are."

Popey smiled at both of them. "I think it's what we were made to be. But what if…" He scooted forward almost ferociously, and then dropped his arms calmly. "What if we were held together differently, knotted up by a rope that doesn't really exist – but is in our hearts and minds?"

Emily and Lilly were both confused, and Emily wanted to see where this went. "Popey, go on, we're listening."

Popey spoke carefully. "It's just that… I wanted to get everyone working together. As long as it was all about the same dream, to keep our home, we worked together. But then I had a different dream that I thought I needed to follow. What happened to me... out on the path – I think I didn't so much follow my dream as become it. Somehow, none of this is about me anymore, not the same way.

Popey continued after a pause to let his speech sink in. "I was taught to realize my dreams and become moral. But what if we taught each other to become our dreams and to realize our own morality? We would work together because we would know it was the right thing to do."

Lilly was not getting it. "But Popey, don't you see how we have to know the magic the Giants have, and how they use it?"
Popey sat back. "We do have to know them, yes. But we don't have to be like them. Not in our hearts."
Emily cut into the conversation hard. "And Popey, can you skip forward a page... there at the bottom. Can you read that?"
Popey fumbled with the book, and found what Emily was pointing to. He read it aloud as clearly and confidently as he could.

"In the end, the only real magic that is important is teaching. Every chance you get, in every smile that shows you are happy with your life, you must teach. There comes a time when you must look beyond the mundane and see the obvious. Take a strong half-step back, and be a part of them both. Not everyone can do this on their own, so you must help them. Teach them the way out of their despair. Teach them the way of life."

CHAPTER 20:
NOTHING AND NOT

As Popey breathed out slowly, all he could feel was his heart pounding. All other emotions had drained out of him for a moment.

Suddenly, he announced to the others, "I'm going to go out. The air in here is a bit thick." He stood up, in silence, and walked out of the door into the wet, heavy air outside. It was still light, but barely. The sun was setting over the river, and the surface crackled orange with the churning current.

In a moment, Emily joined him outside. She said nothing at first, studying Popey's face for a clue. When the silence became unbearable, she finally spoke to him.

"Popey, are you OK?"
"Yeah, I'm fine. In fact, I feel great."
"You look a bit... worried."
"No, I was just thinking about all the time I've spent here."
"Was it happy for you, Popey?" Emily put her arm around his waist, slowly, waiting to see if he would flinch. He didn't.
"I'm just happy I had a chance to step away from all the noise."
"I know what you mean. It's so peaceful here. Is that rain?"
"Yeah, we're getting a little wet. C'mon, follow me."

Popey led Emily to a small, flat rock that stuck out from the hill. He knew it would be a dry place they could watch the rain. When they got there, the rain fell around them like a heavy blanket of water. Popey grinned and stared out into the fabric of drops that cut them off from the rest of the world for a moment.

"Isn't this beautiful, Em?"
"It is, but shouldn't we be in the cave?"
"Why?"
"So that we don't get wet."
"This won't go on long. The sun is still out."
"Are you sure?"

"Nature doesn't make long speeches, Emily. A cloudburst like this doesn't last all day. I don't see why we should go on and on, either."

They said nothing else for a while. The wind splashed them from time to time, pushing them hard against the hill. Soon enough, the rain slowed and their view of the world deepened. The sunset spread out again over the rippling waves of the river. Emily let Popey stand in silence against this beautiful sight for a while, but soon had to say something.

"Popey, what are you thinking now? Are you upset about what we read?"
"No, it's not that. It's just that... I know what I have to do."
"What's that?"
"People who work with the way of the world belong to the world."
"And the rest?"
"People who work with power belong to power. People who work with loss belong to loss. It's up to all of us to be what we want to be."
"And be comfortable with who we are?"
"Yes, exactly." Popey turned to Emily and put his arm around her without thinking. He looked like he was about to kiss her, but just grinned knowingly instead.

"If you give yourself to the way of the world, you'll be a part of the world, Emily. That's what I realized."
"And if you give yourself to power, you are a part of the power."
"Right. If you give yourself to loss, you are lost."
"Is that what you were doing when you came here?"
"Yes. I was trying to get back what I lost. Seems so stupid, really."
"It made sense to you at the time, though. It got you here, and it got you to realize what you needed to see."

Popey thought about that for a moment before responding. "You're right. I figured it out well enough. Just like you did, Em."
"A different way, but we understand each other."
"And the way of the world." He swept his other arm out over the expanse of river that was slowly slipping into darkness.

"Popey, I know it's been long and hard for you."
"Actually, it's been a great adventure."

"So you don't have any regrets at all?"

"Not one. Do you?"

"Me? What would I have to regret?"

"Carrying Misha through that gray place and over the crossing and all those other... hardships."

"Do you still feel guilty for not helping with that?"

"No... a little, yes. I could have helped."

"Well, that was part of my journey. A bit different from yours." She smiled at Popey in the same careless way he had taken to smiling all the time. "But we got to the end together."

They looked at each other a while, and then Popey turned his head to watch the river in one last note of sunset. It was so powerful, and yet so simple. It took its time, but it got where it had to. Popey was the river, just like he was the sunset and the wind and the mud on his feet. He was a part of the way of the world. And he liked that.

Emily felt the silence wrap around them. It was starting to upset her. She spoke carefully as she cut through the quiet with a few simple words.

"Popey, do you trust me?"

"What? Trust? Yes, Emily, I trust you. Why?"

"Do you really trust me?"

Popey turned to look at Emily. "I trust you completely. I trust everything, I think. Do you trust me?"

"Yes, Popey, I do."

"Then what's the matter?"

"I think we should go back to Piketown."

"Why?"

"I just do, Popey. I think we need to."

Popey thought about this for a moment, and nodded his head. Slowly at first, frowning slightly, but soon harder and more happily. "Yes, I agree. Do you think Lilly will want to go?"

"I'm sure she will."

"Then let's go."

"You're comfortable with this?"

"Yes, I am. Very comfortable. Let's pack up and go to Piketown."

Deep down inside, he never felt more comfortable before.

Printed in the United States
38028LVS00004B/1-153